Me & Mr. Bell

by Philip Roy

Cape Breton University Press
Sydney, Nova Scotia, Canada

Cape Breton University Press recognizes the support of the Canada Council for the Arts, Block Grant program, and the Province of Nova Scotia, through the Department of Communities, Culture and Heritage, for our publishing program. Mr. Roy would also like to acknowledge Arts Nova Scotia for including him in its Grants for Individuals program.

We are pleased to work in partnership with these bodies to develop and promote our cultural resources.

Main cover image: Courtesy of the Beaton Institute
Cover layout: Cathy MacLean Design, Chéticamp, NS
Layout: Mike Hunter, Port Hawkesbury and Sydney, NS
First printed in Canada

Library and Archives Canada Cataloguing in Publication
Roy, Philip, 1960-, author
Me & Mr. Bell : a novel / Philip Roy.

ISBN 978-1-927492-55-0 (pbk.)
ISBN 978-1-927492-56-7 (web pdf.)
ISBN 978-1-927492-57-4 (epub.)
ISBN 978-1-927492-58-1 (mobi.)
1. Bell, Alexander Graham, 1847-1922--Juvenile fiction.
I. Title.

PS8635.O91144M45 2013 jC813'.6 C2013-903768-3

Cape Breton University Press
PO Box 5300, Sydney, Nova Scotia, B1P 6L2 Canada

Acknowledgements

Many thanks to Marianne Ward for her excellent editorial work on this book, and thanks to Mike Hunter for overseeing the whole project. I am blessed to have the daily support and inspiration of my wife, Leila (and furry Fritzi); my wonderful kids, Julia, Peter, Thomas (and partner, Lydia), and Julian; my sister, Angela; my darling mother, Ellen; and closest friends, Chris, Natasha and Chiara. And thanks to Jake, to whom this book is dedicated.

For Jacob Gibbons-Cook, who inspired me with his compassion and integrity.

Chapter 1

It was spring 1908. I had just turned ten. The world famous inventor, Alexander Graham Bell, was returning to Baddeck on the steamer. My father, who said that Mr. Bell was the smartest man alive, told me to run down the hill to the McLeary farm with a message. Mr. McLeary would give me a message to carry back. This was an important task, my father said. Could he trust me with it?

I thought it over. All I had to do was hold the message in my hand and run down the hill, cross a field and run down another hill until I reached the McLeary farm, about half a mile away. Then I would run back. That didn't sound too hard, so I said yes. My father sat down and wrote out the message very carefully, folded it and handed it to me. Then he held my arm and looked me in the eye. "You can do this, Eddie, can you?"

I could tell how important it was to my father by the feel of his hand on my arm. It was the first time he had ever asked me to carry a message to someone. I nodded my head obediently.

"Can you?" he asked again to be sure.

"Yes, Sir."

"Good then. Off you go."

I went out the door and ran down the hill.

The McLeary house sat between our house and the lake. It looked like a matchbox from far away. When you came closer, it spread out like open drawers in a bureau. Mr. McLeary built it himself a few years ago, but he put it halfway up the hill instead of on top of it, and the rain ran down the hill and pooled around the house. So he dug a ditch behind the house to draw the water away. But he steered the ditch into the field where he kept his cows, and the extra water turned the field into such a mucky mess that the cows slipped and fell, and one of them broke its leg and he had to kill it before he wanted to. Then he had to build a fence to keep the cows in one part of the field. Every time I saw him out in his field, he was cursing the cows and cursing the hill and the rain and the sky.

My boots beat like a drum when I walked across the porch. Mrs. McLeary met me at the door. "Hello there, young Eddie. What brings you down here all by yourself? Did your mom send you for sugar?"

Mrs. McLeary was nice enough, but she never seemed to be really paying attention.

"No, Mrs. McLeary. My father sent me. He told me to give this to Mr. McLeary." I showed her the note.

"John! There's a message for you from Donald MacDonald."

Mr. McLeary came into the kitchen. He was a big man and his face was always red. He had never spoken to me before. "A message for me, is there?"

"It's from Donald MacDonald."

I could tell from her voice that that was supposed to mean something, but I didn't know what it was. Mr. McLeary looked down at me with eyes that reminded me of a cow. They were big, fat and worried. "Well? Where is it?"

I raised my arm. He took the message out of my hand and crushed my fingers when he did it. He opened the paper and frowned hard and squinted. "What does it say?"

I swallowed hard. I didn't know what it said; I only knew it was about Mr. Bell. Mrs. McLeary peeked over his shoulder. "Ah, he's askin' about Mr. Bell. When he's comin.'"

"When he's comin'?"

I nodded now that I knew what it was about.

Mr. McLeary looked at me as if I was the one who had written the message. "He's comin' tonight!"

"He knows he comin' tonight, John," said Mrs. McLeary. "He wants to know what time he's comin.'"

Mr. McLeary frowned even more. "He's comin' at eight! Tell him he's comin' at eight."

"You'd better write it down, John. The lad might not remember it right."

Mr. McLeary held his breath and turned a shade of purple. "What's to remember? He's comin' at eight!"

"Write it down, John."

"Ah, lordy!"

He fumbled around in his overalls until he found a short pencil, then handed it to me. "Here! Write this down. He's comin' at eight!"

I stared up at him. Did he mean for me to write it?

"Write it!" he barked at me. "He's comin' at eight!"

He pulled at his suspenders and turned away. Mrs. McLeary was busy in the kitchen. I felt awkward standing there by myself.

"Did your mom send you for sugar, Eddie?"

I turned and looked over at her. Mrs. McLeary was kneading dough for bread, and her head was down. She had already asked me that, and I had answered her. I didn't know if I should answer again. "No, Mrs. McLeary, my father—"

"Oh, that's right. Did you write it down?"

"Not yet, Mrs. McLeary."

I held the paper in my left hand and the pencil in my right. I would rather have used my left hand to write because my left hand was better at everything, but I couldn't. You weren't allowed to write with your left hand. You could hold things with it, carry things with it, eat and comb your hair with it, but not write with it. I didn't know why.

On the paper, my father's handwriting looked beautiful, like waves in the lake when it's windy and the water curls a million times the same way, except every now and then there was a fancy shape, as if a seal had stuck its head out of the water, spun around in a somersault and dove back down. The look of my father's handwriting made me feel proud of him.

I knew Mr. Bell was coming at eight, so I figured I wouldn't have to write out the whole sentence. I could just write the word *eight*. But for some reason I had a really hard time remembering how to spell words. In my head, it was as clear as could be. I just thought of the number eight and I knew what it was – eight cows, eight trees, eight apples, eight people – eight was exactly eight, and I knew that as perfectly as I knew anything. The problem was when I tried to write it down. Something got in the way in my mind, and I felt confused and had to concentrate really hard for the simplest thing. I didn't know why that was, and I never told anybody. I avoided writing as much as possible.

But I did remember something important about the number eight that we had learned in school, that it didn't have the letter *a* in it, even though it sounded like it did. It had an *e*. I always thought that was strange. I also knew it had a *t* in it. So, I put those letters down. But I wasn't sure what else went in it. Something told me there was an *h* too, so I made an *h*. But I always confused *h* with *n* because they looked the same to me the way my teacher wrote them, except that one of them had a longer stick than the other. I just couldn't remember which one.

"Are you done?" said Mrs. McLeary. "Your father will be waitin' on you. You'd better scoot."

"Okay."

I handed the pencil to Mrs. McLeary, went out the door and ran back up the hill. My father was waiting. He took the note from my hand, read it and stared at me. "You gave it to Mr. McLeary, did you?"

I nodded.

"And this is all he gave you back?"

"Yes, Sir."

"Well, he's a man of few words, isn't he?"

I just stared at my father. I didn't know what to say. I didn't know how to explain everything the way it happened at the McLeary house.

"Okay then, Eddie. Thank you. Sweep the barn before dark, will you?"

"Yes, Sir."

I went into the barn, picked up the broom and started sweeping. I enjoyed sweeping the barn clean. It gave me a feeling of satisfaction. I was feeling especially happy this night because I had run an errand for my father successfully. It made me feel smart.

It didn't last long.

Chapter 2

The steamer arrived shortly before eight. A small crowd of locals gathered to welcome Mr. Bell back. They clapped when he stepped onto the dock, and shook his hand and wished him well. My father was not there. He arrived half an hour before ten, when the dock was in darkness and no one else was there. He waited for an hour, staring across the water for any sign of the boat. Then he came home, kicked the post of my bed and woke me up. I had never seen him so angry before. I hardly even recognized him. He waved the message in his hand as if it were on fire. "How could you be so *stupid*?"

I didn't know what to do. For a second I wondered if he was going to hit me. He had never hit me before, but some of my friends had been hit by their fathers. Maybe this was the first time it would happen to me. I lay still while he stared at me, his eyes wild with frustration and anger. I didn't understand why it was so important to meet the steamer, and I couldn't stand the way he was staring at me. It seemed like he was trying to make up his mind about something. He looked so disappointed.

It was the way he had looked when it rained all through the month of July the year before, when the hay was ruined. He dropped his head and shook it from side to side, like a horse that didn't want to wear the bridle. Suddenly I wished he would hit me instead of staring at me like that, because it felt like he didn't recognize me, as if I wasn't even his son anymore. I couldn't stand it. Then he left the room. A shiver went up my spine, and I pulled the covers tight around me. I didn't understand what had just happened; I just knew that it was bad.

In the morning, my father pretended not to see me. He walked right by me as if I wasn't even there. I turned to my mother, and she looked like she was trying to make up her mind about something, too. After my father went to the barn, she told me to sit at the table and gave me a pencil and a piece of paper. "You're a smart boy, Eddie, I know you are. Now, I want you to write out the word *eight*."

"Write it?"

She smiled, but I could see that she was frustrated.

"Now, why would you ask me that? I just told you. Aren't you listening?"

"Yes."

"Okay then, write it out."

I stared at the paper and the pencil.

"Pick it up," she said.

I picked up the pencil, but couldn't remember how to hold it for writing; I was too upset. I felt like I was going to cry.

"Write it, Eddie. Write the word. I know you can."

I stared at my mother's hands. They were always wrinkled after she did the washing. And when they weren't wrinkled, they were dry and had thin cracks that sometimes bled. Her hands were so strong. My father's hands were strong, but so were my mother's. I wondered if she would understand that I couldn't remember how to hold the pencil. She was the only one who might.

"Write it, Eddie!"

I looked up at her. My lips were shaking, and I was doing everything not to cry.

"I can't."

She frowned. "What do you mean, you can't? Of course you can. Don't be stubborn, Eddie. It's not a good way to be. You've been to school a long time now; I know you can write the word *eight*. It's not that hard."

"I can't remember...." My voice was breaking.

"Oh, come on now, don't be silly. Put the pencil against the paper and write it. It's just a simple word, Eddie. Don't be stubborn. Everyone can write the word *eight*."

She was right. Everyone could write that word. It was simple. It had to be. I pressed the pencil against the paper and pushed it up. It made a mark, but I couldn't remember where to take it next, and I just drew a line that looked like a tree with only one branch. My mother leaned over my shoulder and looked at what I had done. She stared at the page as if she were staring at a loaf of bread that didn't rise, that came out of the oven like a block of wood. Then she stood up straight and took a deep breath the way she did at church when the priest was finally finished talking, and we could go home. "Lord Almighty, your father was right."

After that, my family treated me differently. My older sister and younger brother took the trouble to show me how to write, and each thought that if only they showed me how, I would be able to do it, like them. I thought so, too. But I couldn't. And they got frustrated. Then my sister explained that it was just as if I had a lame leg or something like that. I was a learning cripple. That's how I should look at it. My brother said that I was just being stubborn, because that's what he heard my mother say. Then my mother said that there were lots of farmers who couldn't read or write, so I needn't worry; I could always be a farmer or work for a farmer, but I probably couldn't be anything else. I wondered if I would be happy being a farmer. I wouldn't mind, I guessed. Most people were farmers. But there was a small nagging feeling inside of me – what if I didn't want to be a farmer? What if I wanted to be something else? What would I do then? Luckily, I didn't have to worry about that yet; I was only ten.

My family talked to me differently, too. They slowed down when they spoke and explained things more carefully than they needed to. At first, I thought it was silly, but I quickly got used to it. We all did. Sometimes they would get impatient trying to explain something, especially my brother, and I would have to finish it for him, but we all got used to the idea that I was a learning cripple and never questioned it anymore. My father still expected me to do my chores, but he never asked me to run an errand for him again, and he started teaching my younger brother things that he didn't teach me.

My father didn't believe as my mother did, that a farmer didn't need to read and write. He thought that the most important thing a man could do was to read about the world and become smart, whether he was a farmer or a fisherman or a priest. And he took great pride in the fact that the smartest man in the world lived in our community, just a few miles away, even though he had never met him. Why he gave up on me so quickly, I never knew. I had never thought of my father as someone to give up easily.

The thing that bothered me the most was when my mother came to the school and explained to the teacher, in front of all of my friends, that I had a problem with learning and that the teacher shouldn't expect as much from me anymore, because it wasn't fair to me. The teacher nodded her head as if she knew all about it and never even said a word to me. She told my mother that she had known there was something wrong all along but never said anything about it, because she was just waiting for me to catch up.

My friends pretended nothing was different when we were outside of school, but in class they made funny faces and rolled their eyes at me. And I didn't like that the boys who were never as smart as me before suddenly thought they were smarter. I still got bored in class waiting for them to understand math, and I stared out the window when the teacher was explaining things to them that I already understood. They still asked me questions about how things worked when we were outside in the field. But in the classroom they could write things that I couldn't, and that seemed to be the most important thing. And they liked to come and show me their work and tell me that I should do it just like them. In my mind, I knew I was smarter. But I couldn't show it.

For a long time, this was how things were and how I thought they would always be. Summer came and went. We started a new school year. And then one day, I met a man who changed everything.

Chapter 3

The first time I met Mr. Bell, I was crossing a field and he was coming down the hill. There was no one else around. It was cloudy, but the air was warm. I wasn't walking anywhere in particular, just crossing the field and feeling the grass with my hands. Dandelions were sticking out of the grass like soldiers with bright yellow helmets. I was always amazed that where the grass was short, the dandelions were short. Where the grass was long, the dandelions were tall. I figured they had to keep up with the grass if they wanted to get any of the sunshine. The cows loved to eat them.

Mr. Bell came charging down the hill like a bear in a wool suit that was too small for him. I knew it was him even though I had never seen him before. He was tall, big and round and had a white bushy beard. He didn't look like a farmer; a farmer would never have such a big belly. It didn't seem to slow him down, though. He was talking loudly and waving his arms in the air, but there was nobody beside him. He was talking to himself.

He reached the bottom of the hill and crossed the field as if he didn't even see it. He walked right past me without seeing me, either! I wondered if maybe he was walking in his sleep. But it was the middle of the afternoon.

I followed him. At the end of the field was a pile of stones. I was curious to see if he would stop and go around it, climb over it or maybe walk right into it. He didn't seem to be looking where he was going.

He went right over the rocks without even slowing down. But as he did, a pencil fell out of his pocket. So I ran and picked it up and tried to catch up with him. He was walking fast! I called after him. "Mr. Bell!" He didn't hear me. "Mr. Bell!" Still he didn't hear me. So I shouted. "*Mr. Bell!*" Then he stopped.

He turned around and saw me. He looked confused. He frowned and squinted at me as if he were trying to figure out what I was. I held up the pencil. "You dropped this, Sir."

He took a deep breath and let it out, and I thought I could feel it from twenty feet away. His face changed, like ice melting really fast. He turned from looking like a wild bear to looking like the friendliest person I had ever seen in my whole life. He came toward me, pushing the tall grass out of his way, reached out with fat fingers and took the pencil out of my hand. Then he smiled at me as if I were his best friend. His eyes twinkled under his bushy eyebrows.

"Now, who would you be?"

I didn't know how to answer him, so I said, "Nobody."

"Nobody?" He grinned. "I never met *nobody* before. Are you sure you aren't *somebody*?"

"Well, my name is Eddie."

When I said that, his eyes opened really wide, his cheeks fell and he suddenly looked sad. I wondered what was wrong, but was afraid to ask.

"What did you say your name was?"

"Eddie."

He wasn't smiling now. He looked far away, and he looked sad.

"Eddie. Ah … my little brother was called Eddie. He died a long time ago, the poor fellow. A day doesn't go by I don't think of him."

I didn't know what to say, so I said, "I have a brother, too."

He stared at me and started smiling again. "Well, shake my hand, young Eddie. I'm Alec Bell. I'm pleased to make your acquaintance."

"I'm pleased to make your acquaintance, Sir." I stuck out my hand, and he shook it. His hand was large, hot and sweaty. Then he nodded his head at me, winked, turned around and walked away, pushing the grass and dandelions out of his way. I stood and watched him go. I was excited now. I had just met the smartest man in the world.

When I came in for supper and told my mother that I had met Mr. Bell, she made a face at me and told me to stop telling stories. I said that I wasn't; I had really met him. She looked up from the stove where she was mashing potatoes. "Where?"

"In the field above MacDougall's."

She frowned into the pot. "I don't think it was Mr. Bell, Eddie, it must have been somebody else. Mr. Bell wouldn't be out walking in MacDougall's field."

"It was him! He told me his name, and he shook my hand."

"He shook your hand?" My mother smiled. She liked the thought that I had shaken hands with Mr. Bell. She turned her head and stared out the window for just a second, and she looked a little dreamy. Then she scooped the potatoes into a bowl. "You'd better wash up." She leaned closer and spoke to me as if she were telling me a secret. "Better not tell your father about that, Eddie."

I saw the look of confusion on her face. "Okay."

At school, no one believed me, and I wished I had never said anything. But I couldn't help it, and it kind of slipped out. Our teacher, Miss Lawrence, seemed to have two faces: one with which she believed everything you said and one with which she didn't believe anything you said. When Joey MacDougall said that he and his father saw Mr. Bell out in a boat with another man, smoking cigars and creating a cloud of fog, I let it slip that I had just met Mr. Bell in the field, and that he shook my hand.

"Yeah, sure he did," said Joey. "And was he standing on four legs and chewing his cud?"

Everybody laughed.

"I did!" I said, and looked toward Miss Lawrence, but her face had suddenly turned from belief to disbelief. After that, I went to MacDougall's field every day for two weeks but never saw Mr. Bell. The next time I met him was down at the lake, when he snuck up on me.

I was standing in the water up to my knees. There was no wind and the lake was flat and shiny, like a silver plate. But I knew it wasn't really flat because the earth is round. That means that everything on the earth is round, even the lake. I had heard that at the ocean you could watch a ship sink below the horizon as it sailed away and that that showed you the roundness of the earth. Well, I wanted to know if I could see any of the roundness of the earth by looking ten miles across Bras d'Or Lake.

So I rolled up my pants, crouched down in the water and brought my head close to the surface, which was kind of awkward. It would have been easier to walk up to my neck and look straight across the lake, but I didn't want to get my clothes all wet. There was a small boat in the distance, and I stared at it, trying to see if it was dropping below the horizon. I was pretty sure it was. But the stones were slippery, and I thought I'd better get a stick to hold on to so I wouldn't fall in. When I turned around, I got a fright. About ten feet behind me, Mr. Bell was crouching the same way I was and was staring out at the lake. He scared the heck out of me.

He was squinting really hard, trying to see whatever it was I was looking at. He was so curious, he was behaving like one of my friends might behave except that none of my friends was *that* curious.

"Heavens above! You'll have to tell me, dear boy," said Mr. Bell, "what you have been staring at so intensely."

I was shy about telling him. "Um … I was trying to see the roundness of the earth on the lake, Sir."

Mr. Bell stood right up. "I knew it! I just knew that was it!" He wore a great big smile now. "And pray, tell me, did you see it?"

I nodded my head. "I think so, Sir."

"Splendid!"

Mr. Bell walked into the water and stood beside me. "That boat way out there?"

"Yes, Sir."

He blocked the sun with his hand and stared. "If only we had some way to measure it."

I wondered if he was being serious. He sure sounded serious. He sounded like he really wanted to know.

"I saw in a math book that you can measure distances between far places if you know what the angles are between them, but I'm not sure how to do it." I knew what angles were, but didn't know how to measure them. I knew that he would know.

Mr. Bell frowned. "Yes, well, mathematics has never been my strong point."

I thought he was joking. How could the smartest man in the world not be good at math? I wanted to ask him what he meant, but was afraid to. He looked at me and must have read my mind. "I always get someone else to work out the math." He winked.

"But...."

"You're wondering how someone can be good at inventing and not be good at math, are you?"

"Yes, Sir."

"Well, it's because being an inventor hasn't got anything to do with being good at math or reading or writing or anything like that. It's about having a good imagination. Inventing is like ... daydreaming. In fact, that's exactly what it is. Then you try to turn your daydreams into something real. And that is just plain hard work. If you put daydreams and hard work together, you get inventions, simple as that." He looked at me and smiled, and his eyes sparkled. "But your daydreams have to be pretty good ones, and you have to work hard for a very long time. That's the part that confounds most people. And what do you want to be when you grow up, Eddie?"

I was surprised that Mr. Bell remembered my name. "I'll probably be a farmer," I said. "I can't seem to learn to read or write very well, but my mom said I could still be a farmer."

Mr. Bell raised his eyebrows. "Is that right? And do you want to be a farmer?"

"I don't know. I guess so, if I have to."

Mr. Bell snorted loudly out of his nose, like a horse. "And who told you that you can't learn to read and write?"

"Everybody."

"Is that so? Well, I have the feeling that I've met this *everybody* before, and it seems to me he's been wrong quite a few times. Have you ever heard of Helen Keller?"

"Yes, Sir."

"Well, I think you should meet her the next time she comes to visit. Helen has become quite a good writer herself, even though she can't see or hear. What do you think of that?"

"She can't see or hear at all?"

"Not even the tiniest bit."

I tried to imagine what that was like, but it just confused me. How could someone not see *and* not hear?

How would she communicate with anyone? It didn't make any sense. Wouldn't she be completely alone in the world? Mr. Bell was staring at me, waiting for an answer.

"I don't understand, Sir. If she is blind and deaf, how does she communicate with anyone?"

"I'll show you." Mr. Bell reached out and put his hand on my face. I shut my eyes. I felt his big fat fingers touching my mouth. It was weird. "Okay. Now, say something, but don't say it out loud."

I did as he told me. I felt his fingers on my mouth as I spoke the words silently.

"You just said, 'The world is round.'"

"Yes, Sir."

He took his hand away. "We learn because we want to learn, Eddie. Nothing in the world can stop us if we want it enough. The *everybody* you were talking to was simply wrong."

I was amazed, but I was also curious about something else and hoped he wouldn't mind if I asked him. "What is it that you want the most, Mr. Bell?"

Mr. Bell looked at me as if he were surprised at my question, then burst out laughing. "Oh, too many things to count, my dear boy. I want *everything* the most." Then he stared across the lake with the most determined look on his face. "Carrying people through the air on a flying ship – just like a sailing ship on the sea – that's one of them. And we're close now."

Mr. Bell put his hand on my shoulder and squeezed it. "Any boy smart enough to look for the roundness of the earth on the lake is smart enough to learn to read and write." Then he winked at me and walked away. I watched him go.

On my way home, I thought about everything he said. This time, I wasn't in a hurry to tell anyone I had met Mr. Bell. They would just say I was making it up. And who would believe that he talked about inviting me to come to his house to meet Helen Keller? No one. I still found it hard to believe that Helen Keller could write when she couldn't see or hear. Mr. Bell said that she had become a really good writer. How? I couldn't get my head around it.

Chapter 4

One time, a calf was born blind in the barn. I remembered it. As soon as it took a breath of air, it died. My mother clicked her tongue and said that it was one of nature's mistakes. My father stared at it with confusion and frustration. He tied a rope around its legs and used a horse to drag it out to the woods. The mother followed it out. I never knew that nature could make mistakes; I thought it was perfect. It was something I was going to ask Mr. Bell if I ever got the chance to meet him again.

How could anyone live if they couldn't see *and* couldn't hear? It made me so curious I took a candle and went into the barn, rubbed the candle wax between my fingers until it was soft and stuck it into my ears. Then I covered my eyes with two rags and tied a belt around my head to hold them tight. Now I couldn't hear or see. What a strange feeling it was. The first thing I noticed was that I could smell the hay better. I took a couple of steps and felt the floor beneath my feet. You could still tell a lot of things by touching and smelling. I started moving forward slowly with my hands stuck out straight, careful not to trip over anything. But I knew the barn really well, so it wasn't the same as being deaf and blind in a strange place.

I was thinking of going somewhere else when my foot hit something, and I fell forward and hit the floor really hard. It scared me because I couldn't see myself falling, and it felt as if the floor had jumped up and hit me. I got to my knees and felt around. I had tripped over the broom handle. Suddenly, I felt a tug at my shoulder. Someone was beside me. It must have been my brother. "What do you want?" I said, but couldn't hear his answer and couldn't tell how loud I was talking. He tugged harder. "Smarten up!" I said. Then I got an idea. I reached out and felt for his face. I wanted to place my fingers over his mouth and feel what he was saying. But he slapped my arm away roughly and ripped the belt and rags from my head. It wasn't my brother; it was my father.

"What happened, Eddie? Who did this to you? Did your friends tie you up?"

"No, Sir."

"Then who tied a belt around your head?"

"I did."

He stared at me, trying to understand. How could I explain to him what I was doing? I didn't know, but figured I'd better try. "I was trying to find out what it was like to be deaf and blind, like Helen Keller."

I wondered if he was going to get angry. He didn't. His face softened and so did his voice. "My son, you are going to need all the brains you've got. Do you hear me? Don't make your life more difficult than it is by taking away your sight and hearing. I know who Helen Keller is, and I don't imagine she's anybody you'd want to be. Do you understand me?"

"Yes, Sir."

He looked me sternly in the eye. "Do you understand me, Eddie?"

"Yes, Sir."

"Good then. Carry the sledgehammer down to Mr. McLeary, will you?"

"Okay."

"And … sweep the barn afterward, okay?"

"Okay."

The barn didn't need sweeping. He just didn't know what else to say to me. I didn't mind. I was glad he was trusting me with an errand again, even if it was just carrying a sledgehammer down the hill. I picked up the hammer and went out of the barn.

I once heard my mother say that Mr. McLeary was not burdened with common sense. I didn't know what she meant by that when she said it, but eventually I figured it out. Like other men in our community, including my father, Mr. McLeary had taken to smoking a pipe because Mr. Bell smoked a pipe, so people figured it must make you smarter. Some of the older farmers already smoked a pipe, and I never heard anyone say that they were smarter.

I watched Mr. McLeary lighting his pipe outside his house on my way to school one morning but didn't think he was doing it right. He raised his eyebrows at me the way he always did now because I was a learning cripple, but I noticed a whole pile of burnt matches on the ground by his feet. From the way he was puffing his cheeks, I was pretty sure he was blowing into his pipe instead of sucking on it. Then, later in the morning, we smelled smoke at school. Everyone ran outside and saw a dark cloud over the McLeary farm. On the way home, I saw that a whole corner of his hayfield was burnt. A handful of farmers were there, drinking tea and eating cookies that Mrs. McLeary had made for them for putting out the fire. Everyone was saying how smart Mr. McLeary had been to alert the other farmers before the fire had reached his house and how clever he had been to discover it so quickly in the first place. No one knew how the fire could have started, but Mrs. McLeary said it must have been a freak of nature. The very next day, I saw Mr. McLeary lighting his pipe at the well. As he took a deep breath, he coughed, and the pipe slipped out of his mouth. He swung at it as if he were trying to catch a ball but missed, and the pipe fell down the well. Then he saw me and raised his eyebrows again, but the look on his face was the look of a frightened cow.

I carried the sledgehammer down the hill. Mr. McLeary was standing in his field with a tired look on his face. It had rained a lot. His fence was leaning over. His cows kept sliding into it when they came in and out of the field. I saw his sledgehammer in the mud and it had a broken handle. He must have hit the fence posts too hard trying to drive them deeper into the ground. He looked really tired when he saw the sledgehammer in my arms. He wouldn't even look me in the face. I stared at the cow path. It was stirred into brown soup. Cows will follow the same path no matter what. Suddenly, I got an idea. "Fill it with stones," I said. I just blurted it out because he looked so desperate and didn't know what to do.

Mr. McLeary glared at me. "What?"

"Fill the path with stones. It'll give the cows something to walk on."

He made a face as if I had just said the dumbest thing in the world. Then he turned and stared at the path. Then he turned and stared at his hayfield, where there were huge piles of stones on the sides. He stuck out his arm, and I passed him the sledgehammer. It was so heavy I had to use two arms just to hold it, but he took it in one hand as if it didn't weigh anything at all.

"Thank your daddy," he said roughly.

"Okay." I turned around and walked away. I waited to hear the sound of the sledgehammer crashing into a post, but it never came. The next morning, on my way to school, I saw Mr. McLeary pushing a wheelbarrow full of stones into the field. I think he saw me, but he pretended he didn't. By the end of the week, he had created a wide stone lane across his field. It looked really good. His cows came in and out without slipping. I heard my mother and father talk about it. They thought he had been clever. On my way to school, I saw Mr. McLeary standing on the lane, looking proud of the stone path. He still raised his eyebrows at me.

Chapter 5

Miss Lawrence had brown hair and brown eyes and every day she wore the same brown dress, brown shoes and brown coat to school. She came inside, unbuttoned her coat, hung it up on the coat rack, took a handkerchief out of her pocket and squeezed it into her sleeve. And it stayed there all day and never fell out. The only change she ever made was once she sewed a patch over a hole in her coat. At first the patch was darker brown than the rest of her coat, but by the end of the year it was the same colour.

We studied math first thing every morning. I liked math. I found it easy when the exercises were read out loud and I could do them in my head. Most of my friends were the opposite; they couldn't do it in their heads – they needed to see it written down on the page. Sometimes they would ask for my help, if they were really stuck. They would tell me the question out loud, and I would give them the answer. But no one gave me credit for being smart, because I couldn't read the questions.

After math we had reading, which was usually pretty boring. Miss Lawrence always stood perfectly still in front of the class while she read to us. Sometimes I imagined that she was a talking tree. I daydreamed *a lot* in school. I couldn't help it. My mind liked to wander.

Then one day, Miss Lawrence opened a new book, and everything changed for me. She started to read about ancient Greece. I didn't know why, but everything about ancient Greece interested me. My friends thought it was boring, but I couldn't get enough of it. It became the most interesting thing I ever learned in school.

In ancient Greece, it was always hot and sunny. People would sit around on hills, in the daytime or at night, where it was always warm, and ask interesting questions and tell great stories. The ocean was green, or blue, and sparkled with flecks of gold. There were olive trees, orange trees, lemon trees and cherry trees. There were pink mountains with golden temples on top and dry, dusty plains that stretched forever and sun-baked beaches where the sand shone like gold and probably had gold in it.

There were gods and goddesses, like Apollo and Athena, and heroes like Hercules, Achilles and Odysseus. There were rulers, like Alexander the Great, and philosophers who walked around outside and asked important questions, like Plato, Aristotle and Socrates. There were writers, like Homer, who was blind, and mathematicians, like Archimedes.

Of all of them, the one who fascinated me the most was Archimedes, because he invented tools that gave the power of a hundred men to just one person. Even to a boy.

And you didn't have to be a god or a ruler or a hero. You could be an ordinary person. While my friends yawned and rolled their eyes, I listened to every word Miss Lawrence read as if it carried magic power. Because it did.

But then, Miss Lawrence passed the book around and made everyone read a little bit of what she had just read, and that just about ruined it for me. Nobody could read it as well as she did. Nobody could say the names right. And when it was my turn, I couldn't read it at all and had to fake it, which was what I always did at reading time – I tried really hard to remember what she had read, then sort of made it up. And no one cared because no one was paying that much attention in the first place, and nobody expected me to get it right. When *we* read it, it took the magic right out of it.

The first day that Miss Lawrence read from the book, I asked if I could stay in for lunch and look at it by myself, but she said no, go outside and play. The second day, she just stared at me, looked kind of frustrated, but said, okay, read for a little while, then go outside. I said thank you. I didn't actually want to read the book; I just wanted to look at the pictures.

Some of the pictures showed pulleys, wheels, ropes, ramps and arrows pointing in every direction. One picture showed a small man lifting a heavy stone block off the ground just by pulling down on a rope. There were pictures of old men and their names, but I couldn't tell who was who, except that the man next to the pulleys was probably Archimedes. All of the men were old and had white beards, just like Mr. Bell. He would fit in perfectly. At the top of the diagrams of pulleys were two long words. When I gave Miss Lawrence back the book, I asked her what they said.

"Applied Mathematics."

"What does it mean?"

She frowned at me and sighed. "Why are you so interested in that, Eddie? It means when you use mathematics to move things around." She picked up the pointer, reached up and stabbed a book on the top shelf of the bookcase. "That's *Applied Mathematics*. But it's way over your head, Eddie. It's too hard for most people to understand."

"Does it have pictures in it?"

"I don't know. I've never opened the book."

"Thank you, Miss Lawrence." That's what I thought. Applied mathematics was a kind of magic that let you move heavy things around as if they weighed nothing. It was a kind of magic that was real. Who wouldn't be interested in that?

I stared at the big book on the shelf and wondered if it had pictures in it. It bothered me so much that I couldn't read. And it didn't make sense. Why would I be so good at math but so terrible at reading and writing? I thought about it all the way home from school. At home, I took my school book, scribbler and pencil, sat on my bed and decided to teach myself how to read and write. If Helen Keller could learn to write, then so could I. First I would teach myself how to write numbers, then other things after that. The number I wanted to start with was *eight*.

I opened my school book, found the numbers list and copied out the word *eight*. It had five letters. That seemed easy enough. I copied the word exactly as it was in the book. Then I turned to another page in my scribbler and wrote it out ten times. Then I compared my writing with the word in the book. I couldn't believe it – I had spelled it wrong six times! Six times, I wrote *eihgt* instead of *eight*. They looked the same to me. It was only when I went from letter to letter with the pencil that I saw the difference.

Okay, I thought, I'll try it again. So I did. This time, I got it wrong only twice. That was better, but I still couldn't believe I had spelled it wrong at all. And it was tiring. It was easier to run all the way across the field and back than it was to write out a number twenty times. At least writing the letters down so many times made me feel confident that I would remember the difference now between *h* and *n* – *h* had a long stick and *n* had a short one, like in the word *no*.

Next I practised writing the number *one*. As I stared at it, I wondered why it didn't start with a *w*. Shouldn't it? It sounded like it did. I said the word slowly and carefully. Yes, it definitely sounded like a *w*. But there wasn't a *w* in the word. Why did we have a *w* if we didn't always use it? That didn't make sense at all. But *one* only had three letters and was fairly easy to remember. I got it right every time. And that felt good.

I moved on to the number *two*. Words were just shapes, like trees or horses or barns, except that if you added a few pieces of wood to a barn or took a few pieces away, it was still a barn. You wouldn't mistake it for a tree or a horse. And if you took a branch away from a tree or a leg away from a horse, you would still know it was a tree and a horse. You wouldn't think it was a barn. But if you made even the tiniest change to a word, it wasn't the same word anymore. It became something else. I had already learned that the hard way.

As I stared at the word *two*, I saw something I couldn't believe. It had a *w* in it! But you didn't pronounce it. Now this was crazy. Why would one word be missing the letter that you spoke and the next word be using it when you didn't speak it? I didn't know who invented our language, but this seemed pretty stupid to me. How were you supposed to remember that?

After practising just three words, I was exhausted. I wanted some fresh air, so I went outside, crossed the yard and climbed the fence behind the barn. I picked up some rocks and threw them at the fence post. This was something I was good at, and it felt good. After I threw about twenty-five rocks and hit the post sixteen or seventeen times, I went back in the house. But just before I did, I took a sharp rock and scratched the word *eight* into the wall of the barn. It was a word I would never forget.

Back inside my room, I sat down and stared at the number *three*. I had a nagging feeling inside. Had I put the *g* and *h* in the right order on the barn? I thought I had but wasn't sure. I sat on my bed and tried to continue studying, but it was bugging me so much I couldn't concentrate. I had to know. So I took my school book outside to compare. As I stared at the back of the barn, then looked into the book, I saw that the word scratched into the wood was spelled wrong. I stared at it for a long time. It felt as if someone, somewhere, or maybe the whole world even, was trying to tell me something. And what they were trying to tell me was that it was hopeless; it really was.

Chapter 6

The third time I met Mr. Bell I was down at the lake on a gloomy, rainy day. I was walking along the beach, picking up shells and stones and throwing them into the water. As I wandered along, I wondered if nature really did make mistakes. Were any of these shells a mistake? Were any of these stones a mistake? What about those waves? Were they all perfect, or were some not as perfect as the others? What was a mistake anyway, something that didn't do what it was supposed to do? Why would a calf be born blind then die? Why did some potatoes grow big and others small? Why were some apples shrivelled up and covered with rough skin? Why was I born with a stronger left hand if I wasn't allowed to use it for writing? Why would I be good at math but hopeless at writing? I stared far out on the lake. It was so dark and gloomy. If nature did make mistakes, could they be fixed?

As I reached the far side of the cove where the beach ended and where the rocks went up the hill into the woods that led to Beinn Bhreagh, the land owned by the Bells, I saw a large man bent over the water, picking up a piece of wood. He looked like one of the locals from a distance. Up close I saw that it was Mr. Bell. He was standing close to the trees, as he if had just snuck out of the woods and didn't want anybody to see him. He looked sleepy. When he saw me, he smiled. I didn't want to bother him, but he waved for me to come over. "Ahoy! Eddie! Come and say hello!"

"Good morning, Mr. Bell."

"Good morning, lad. Have you ever seen a finer morning on the lake?"

I looked at the darkness of the lake to see if I had missed anything. "No, Sir."

"And how does it go, my friend? I can see by the look on your face that you're carrying a weight."

I didn't know anyone could see it in my face. "Mr. Bell, do you believe that nature makes mistakes?"

Mr. Bell stood up straight and stared at me with a look almost of shock, as if I had poked him with a stick. "Nature makes mistakes? Good heavens, my boy, the last time I saw you, you were trying to measure the roundness of the earth. Today, you're considering nature's manufacturability. You're quite the philosopher, my young friend."

"Thank you, Sir." I didn't know why he called me a philosopher, but I didn't mind.

He raised a hand to his beard, and I could tell he was thinking about it. He continued to look surprised. "Does nature make mistakes? Well, I suppose that would be like asking if God makes mistakes, wouldn't it? And I suppose I would have to answer that, no, God doesn't make mistakes. Thus, we would have to conclude that nature doesn't make mistakes either." He furrowed his brow. "But I sense that you are asking this question for a deeper reason than just a passing curiosity. Why do you want to know?"

I dropped my head. "Because I think nature made a mistake with me. I'm good at math, and I think I'm smart enough, but when I try to read or write, it just doesn't work. When I just look at words it feels like a cow is sitting on my head. There must be a mistake somewhere."

He squinted at me. "Yes, you're smart enough; I can see that for myself. Tell me what happened."

So I told him about my attempts to write out numbers. And he listened as carefully as if I had been explaining how the planets moved around the sun. When I finished, he was silent for a while. He was thinking. Finally he said, "How many letters are in the alphabet?"

"Twenty-six."

"What's half of twenty-six?"

"Thirteen."

"What's half of thirteen?"

"Six and a half."

"What's half of that?"

"Um … three and a quarter."

"Okay. And what's a hundred times three and a quarter?"

I had to think about that for a while. Mr. Bell took out a small notepad from his jacket pocket and wrote something down while he waited for me. I recognized his pencil.

"I think it is three hundred and twenty-five, Sir."

"Right you are! Now, how do you spell boat?"

I took a deep breath. I was pretty sure it started with a *b*, because of the sound of it. And it probably ended with a *d* or a *t*; I wasn't sure which. It only had an *o* sound in the middle. "Is it *b-o-d*?"

He twisted his head sideways, but didn't answer. "And how do you spell lake?"

I was glad he was asking me easy words. "I think it's l-a-k."

He rubbed his beard. "Hmmm. And how do you spell dream?"

I closed my eyes and thought about it. I could hear the *e* sound and knew that it must end with an *m*, but I couldn't figure out how it started.

"Does it start with a *j*?"

He shook his head.

"I'm sorry. I don't know."

Mr. Bell frowned. He was thinking hard now. "Let's try something else. See if you can remember these numbers."

"Okay."

"Thirteen … twenty-six … thirty-nine … forty-five … fifty-six. Here, I'll say them again." And he did. I closed my eyes and concentrated hard. "Now, before you try to repeat them, try to remember these letters: *d – r – e – a – m*. I'll repeat them, too." And he did. "Okay. What were the numbers?"

"Thirteen, twenty-six, thirty-nine, forty-five and fifty-six."

"Excellent! And the letters?"

I tried hard to remember. "Um … *d* …." What came next? I didn't know. But I thought I remembered an *m*. "*M*? I can't remember any more of them."

Mr. Bell looked at me beneath his bushy eyebrows and smiled. "Yes, I see what you mean, Eddie. We've got something here that begs looking at." He raised his eyebrows and his face suddenly lit up. "Did you know, recently, we crashed another flying machine?"

"I'm sorry to hear that, Sir."

"Bah! There's nothing to be sorry about. The crash is just a detail, Eddie. The miracle is that we got the thing in the air in the first place. And it was carrying a man! It was a glorious success!" He stared at me to see what I would say. But I didn't know how to answer.

"Before you go any further, Eddie, you must learn to celebrate your successes. You can certainly celebrate that you've got a first-class mind in mathematics. And you're a smart boy, you really are. And you might even consider celebrating that you spelled the word *eight* correctly eight times out of ten. Celebrate your success with it. Don't dwell on your failures." He stopped, pulled on his beard and frowned. "On the other hand, our failures are our friends, too."

"What?" Now he was losing me.

"Well, truth is, we learn quite a lot from our failures. We learn, for instance, what didn't work. This helps us to try something new. In fact, maybe if we didn't have failure at all, we wouldn't keep on trying. We wouldn't work so hard." Now it sounded like Mr. Bell was talking to himself as much as he was talking to me. "And so … as much as we should celebrate our successes, I suppose we have to be grateful for our failures, too. That's a funny thought now, isn't it?"

"Yes, Sir."

"Tell me, Eddie, can you come to our house next week on Saturday, in the afternoon? I would like you to meet a very special lady who will be visiting us then."

I knew he meant Helen Keller. "Yes, Sir. I would love to."

"Good! Come in the early afternoon. We'll be on the porch. Just come up and show yourself, and I'll introduce you to everyone. Will you do that?"

"Yes, Sir. I will. Thank you very much."

"You're welcome. Now, in the meantime, concentrate on celebrating your successes and being grateful for your failures, too. And when we meet next, tell me which you have found more useful to you."

"Yes, Sir, I will."

"Good then." Mr. Bell squeezed my shoulder with his hand, turned around, climbed up the rocks and disappeared into the woods. Under the shadows of the trees, he looked like a bear.

Chapter 7

Every night for a week, I went to bed with excited nervous energy. And it was hard to sleep. I was excited to be invited to the Bells' house at Beinn Bhreagh but got nervous when I thought about actually going there. How should I behave? What would I say? What if I said something stupid, and everyone laughed at me? I promised myself that I would only speak when someone spoke to me. Every night I told myself that over and over until I felt sure that that's what I would do. Still, it was hard to sleep. And I didn't tell anyone I was going, not even my mother or father. I didn't think anyone would believe me anyway, and maybe they'd even try to keep me from going.

When Saturday finally came, I hurried through my chores. I fed the cows, shovelled manure, fed the chickens and collected eggs. I fed the horses, let them out and swept the barn. When we sat down for lunch, I could hardly sit still I was so anxious. My mother noticed it. "Eddie. What's with you today?"

"Nothing."

"You're all fidgety. Are you feeling okay?"

"Yes."

"You're not sick?"

"No, I feel fine."

My father raised his eyes to look at me but didn't say anything. I wondered what he was thinking.

"May I be excused now?"

My father spoke without raising his eyes from his tea. His lips were still touching the cup. "Did you finish all your chores?"

"Yes, Sir."

"Where ya goin'?" asked my brother.

"Nowhere."

"Can I come?"

"No."

"You must be going somewhere," said my sister, "you didn't wait for dessert."

I forgot we were even having dessert. "I'm just not very hungry today."

My mother put her hand on my head and felt for a fever. "You feel a little warm, Eddie. Maybe you should have a lie-down this afternoon."

"No! No, I'm fine. Really, I am. I'm just going out for a walk."

"I know where he's going," said my sister. "He's hoping to run into Mr. Bell again."

"Can I come?" said my brother again.

"No!"

I carried my dishes to the counter and put them down. I grabbed my jacket off the hook, put my boots on and went out the door. "Come back if you start to feel a fever, Eddie!"

"Okay, Mom!"

I went across the yard and into the field. In the field, I took off running as fast as I could until I was out of sight and could look back through the winter wheat and see my brother coming out of the house. I knew he was going to follow me. Now, he couldn't see me. I turned down the hill toward the lake.

It took almost two hours to get to the Bell house. I was afraid I was going to be late. I had never been there before, but I knew where it was. Everyone did. But even though I knew it was the biggest house in Baddeck, nothing prepared me for the size of it. When I came up the lane and caught sight of it, my mouth dropped. It was bigger than our church and bigger than the biggest barn. It was tall and fat, with lots of roofs sticking up in different directions and too many windows to count. It sat on the lawn as if it had grown out of the ground like a gigantic mushroom. On one side, I saw a large porch filled with people. I heard laughter. Now I was really nervous.

I climbed the first step of the porch and was greeted by a very friendly young woman, who was probably one of Mr. Bell's daughters. She reached down and offered me her hand. I wasn't used to shaking a woman's hand, so I just stuck my hand up and gently squeezed her fingers.

"You must be Eddie," she said.

I nodded my head.

"Come up and meet everyone."

She let go of my hand, and I followed her up the steps. There were so many people here I didn't know which way to turn. I looked for Mr. Bell, but there seemed to be two of him. One was standing up, and the other one was lying in a chair with a blanket over his lap. Both were smoking pipes. Both had white hair and bushy beards, but the one who was standing turned to look at me, and I knew it was Mr. Bell. "Ah, young Eddie! Come over and meet everyone. This is my darling wife, Mrs. Bell."

Mrs. Bell offered me her hand, and I took it the way I had taken her daughter's hand. Mrs. Bell squinted and smiled so warmly she reminded me of Mr. Bell right away. She looked like a very special person, like a queen or something. "Hello, Eddie. I am very pleased to make your acquaintance. I have heard that you are a most promising young man. My husband has a gift for surrounding himself with men of talent."

"Thank you, Mrs. Bell. Thank you for inviting me to your home."

She tilted her head and smiled so sweetly her eyes twinkled like Mr. Bell's, although they were smaller. "It is a pleasure."

"And here is my father, the illustrious Mr. Bell," boomed Mr. Bell. I could tell that Mr. Bell was speaking loudly so that his father could hear him. His father put his pipe in his mouth, reached up and shook my hand. "Welcome," he said roughly. His hand was older and shakier and a little smaller than Mr. Bell's hand.

Then Mr. Bell introduced me to his other daughters and to his granddaughters, who were very pretty, and then to Casey Baldwin and Douglas McCurdy, who were friendly, too, and looked very smart. There were a few more people but too many for me to remember their names. I was wondering where Helen Keller was. Maybe she was in the house. Maybe it was too confusing for her to be around so many people.

"Have you ever seen a finer afternoon, Eddie?" said Mr. Bell. I was starting to realize that Mr. Bell found every day better than the one before it.

"No, Sir."

"Here. Have a glass of Nana's famous lemonade." He pointed to a tray that a maid was carrying around the porch. "Have you met everyone?"

"Um … I haven't met Helen Keller yet, Sir."

"Oh, but you did, my boy."

"I did?"

"You did. She greeted you on the step. Here she is again."

I turned around, and standing behind me was the first lady I had met on the steps. She was smiling. "Tell me something about yourself, Eddie," she said, and her hand came up quickly and rested against my mouth.

Chapter 8

Helen Keller's hand pressed lightly against my mouth. Her fingers read my words when I spoke, and then something very amazing happened. All of a sudden I understood what intelligence was. It was like jumping into the lake for the first time and feeling what water felt like when it swallowed you up. Intelligence was a kind of hunger. Helen Keller's touch was soft and gentle, but her determination to know was really hungry and powerful. I felt it. And I knew now that that's what intelligence was – the hunger that the mind has to know things. And this was why she could listen without ears and see without eyes, because her hunger to know was so strong. And I knew that she could do anything she wanted to, because she was so determined. This was the power of intelligence. And she had *a lot* of it. This was the most important lesson I ever learned. In a few seconds of Helen Keller's touch, I learned more than I had learned in all my time at school.

I didn't know what to say, so I told her my name and my age and where I lived. "What else?" she said. "Tell me more." So I told her that I had a problem learning how to read and write. I didn't mind saying it in front of all of these people, because talking with Helen Keller was so special, and I just kind of knew she would understand. She did. "*I* before *e* except after *c*. I like to use rhymes like that to help me remember how to spell. You can make up your own rhymes, too, to help you remember."

"*I* before *e*?"

"Yes. The spelling of words with *i* and *e* in them. The *i* always comes first unless there is a *c* in front of it. For example, the word *chief* has an *i* and an *e*, and the *i* comes first because that's the rule. It's the same for the word *thief*. But in the word *receive*, the *e* comes first because it has a *c* in front of it. Do you understand?"

I was trying really hard, but it was too much and too fast for me. "I think maybe I'll have to practise it."

"Of course! Practice makes perfect! Learning something the first time is like meeting somebody just once. Practising is like becoming good friends. It is a world of difference."

She said *world* as if she were riding on a merry-go-round. "Tell me a word you are struggling to spell."

"Eight."

"Oh, yes. The *g* and the *h*, right?"

"Right."

"Do you like challenges?"

"Challenges?"

"Yes. Do you like to beat your friends in a race?"

"Yes. When I can."

"Well, I challenge you to come up with a rhyme for *g* and *h*. I'll give you a hint: *g* always comes before *h*, just as it does in the alphabet."

"*G always* comes before *h*?"

"Yes, it does. I can't wait to hear your rhyme."

When Helen Keller pulled her hand away from my mouth, the sight and sound of our talk disappeared. Without her touch, there was nothing there. It was as if she had gone into another world. She squeezed my shoulder, turned around and walked across the porch. Her hand reached out for the wall at just the right time. She walked close to the steps without falling and reached down and touched the shoulder of Mr. Bell's father as she went inside. I found it hard to believe that she would really be interested in whatever rhyme I could make, but she sounded like she was.

A maid handed me a glass of lemonade. Another maid gave me a cookie from a plate. I sat on the top step and ate the cookie and sipped the lemonade and smiled at Mr. Bell who was smiling at me but listening to his father. Bees were buzzing close to the steps and small birds were flying in and out of the porch while people chatted and laughed in the warm afternoon sun. I never felt so special in all my life, just being here with these wonderful, friendly people.

While I watched a bee buzz close to my lemonade, I thought of how *bee* rhymed with *g*. If I could find a word to rhyme with *h*, maybe I could make a rhyme. Well I tried, but I couldn't find a single word to rhyme with *h*. But I did think that honey started with *h*, because that's how it sounded. Helen Keller said that *g* always came before *h*, as it does in the alphabet. Well bees came before honey because they made honey, so … "as bees come before honey, *g* comes before *h*." I knew it didn't rhyme, but

I thought it was pretty good anyway. Now I couldn't wait to share it with Helen Keller.

When she came out of the house, I stood up, put my glass on the railing and waited for her to come over. Watching her was really interesting. When she pushed open the screen door and stepped onto the porch, she did everything in the opposite order she had done it on the way in. But this time, when she reached down to touch the shoulder of Mr. Bell's father, he was leaning to the other side, picking through some newspapers. Instead of squeezing his shoulder, her fingers squeezed at air, then touched the chair. She frowned for a second, then she smiled again. I looked to see if anyone noticed, but no one did. She crossed the porch to where I was, but when she reached for the railing, just as she had before, her hand bumped the glass I put down there and it fell into the grass without a sound. I wasn't even sure she knew she had done it, and no one else saw it. In her other hand, she gripped a piece of paper. She seemed a little excited. "Eddie?" She reached out with her hand. I stepped closer. Her fingers touched my forehead, then quickly found my mouth. I answered. "Yes, Miss Keller?"

"I wrote down some words with *g* and *h* so you can practise spelling them."

She passed me the sheet of paper. I took it and stared at it. The words were written with big letters that looked like they were made by someone learning to write letters for the first time. But they were neat and tidy and much better than I could make them.

"There is freight, weight, night, flight, plough, bough, right, fight, ought, fought, mighty, flighty, tight, sight.

That's fourteen. If you learn all of these, I am certain you will never forget the order of *g* and *h*."

I looked up at her. Did she really expect me to learn all of these? She was smiling and looking back at me, but not *exactly* at me. Her eyes were blue and looked perfect. I didn't know then that they were made of glass. "Thank you," I said. "I promise to learn them."

"Wait! I wanted them to rhyme, so you can say them in rhythm, like you're marching. But I need one more." She reached out for the paper, and I passed it to her. She bent down, pressed the paper against her thigh, took the pencil and slowly wrote one more word. It was messier than the others. But … I couldn't believe it … she wrote it with her left hand! Then she started swinging her arms and raising her knees as if she were marching. "Freight, weight, night, flight, plough, bough, right, fight, ought, fought, mighty, flighty, tight, sight and tough!"

Everyone on the porch was clapping, but Helen Keller couldn't see or hear it. "And do you have a rhyme for me yet, young man?"

"I have one, but…." I stopped. Unless her hand was on my mouth, she wouldn't even know I was speaking. Instantly, it appeared. "I made one, but it doesn't rhyme."

"And?"

"As bees come before honey, *g* comes before *h*."

She burst into a smile. "It's perfect! Alec! Alec! Come listen to Eddie's rhyme."

Mr. and Mrs. Bell came over, stood beside Helen Keller and held her hands. "What is happening?" said Mrs. Bell.

Mr. Bell opened Mrs. Bell's hand and tapped with his fingers as if he were tapping on a table. "Go ahead, my boy," he said. "We are listening."

I said my rhyme again.

"Splendid!" said Mr. Bell. "You have got a good teacher." He smiled and tapped in Mrs. Bell's hand again. I couldn't help staring, I was so curious, and he must have seen it on my face. He winked at me. "Yes, dear Mrs. Bell does not hear either, but she can read your lips from across the porch." Mrs. Bell looked sharply into my eyes and smiled at me. She really looked like a queen.

After a while, Mr. Bell announced that he, Casey Baldwin and Douglas McCurdy had pressing duties in the laboratory, but urged everyone else to continue enjoying themselves on the porch. I took that as a sign that I should leave. I went to Helen Keller and touched her hand. She raised it to my mouth, and I thanked her for teaching me, and I promised again to learn her rhyme. She held my face with both hands, reached down and gently kissed me on the forehead. If one photograph was worth a thousand words, then one touch from Helen Keller was worth a thousand photographs.

Chapter 9

Mr. Bell, Mr. Baldwin, Mr. McCurdy and I walked together down the lane toward the laboratory. Mr. Baldwin and Mr. McCurdy were a lot younger than Mr. Bell, and I could tell they wanted to go faster, but they walked at Mr. Bell's pace. Mr. Bell smoked his pipe as we went, and he seemed to be in deep thought. For a few moments, nobody said anything. Then Mr. McCurdy spoke.

"I made a model of it," he said.

"You did?" said Mr. Bell. He raised his eyebrows.

"I'll fly it for you, Doug," said Mr. Baldwin.

"Not likely," said Mr. McCurdy. He was grinning. "I'll be flying that aeroplane myself."

"And the wings?" said Mr. Bell.

"Thin and flat. It's the only way to get the lift we need." He sounded like he was apologizing.

Mr. Bell shook his head. I had the feeling they had talked about this a lot before. "Too dangerous, boys. Sure, you might get into the air, but you've got to stay there. And don't forget, you've got to come down." Mr. Bell raised his eyebrows a little higher and smiled.

"Let me show you the model," said Mr. McCurdy.

"Yes, yes, let's have a look," said Mr. Bell. Now he sounded almost as excited as them.

At the doorway to the laboratory, we stopped. Mr. Bell let the two younger men go in, then looked down at me and took the pipe from his mouth. I was waiting for him to say goodbye. It was time for me to go home, though I didn't want to. But that's not what he said.

"Come in, Eddie! Come in and see what these ambitious young men are up to."

"Okay. Thank you, Mr. Bell." I stepped into the laboratory. I was so glad. I was dying to see the model, too.

The laboratory was just a large shed with windows on one side and tables and benches in the middle. There were tools everywhere and wood and metal against the walls and in the corners. There were wheels, pipes, rolls of canvas, wire, glass bottles, rubber hoses and all kinds of objects and shapes that would be kind of hard to describe. On one end of a long table was the model flying machine. It was about two and a half feet long, made of wood and had rubber wheels. Its wings were even longer and were made of canvas. Mr. Casey and Mr. McCurdy were standing around it, talking excitedly. They had a lot of energy.

Mr. Bell cleaned his pipe before he came over to look closely at the model. Mr. McCurdy waited patiently for him, but I could tell he was anxious for him to see it. Mr. Bell bent down and tapped his pipe into a metal can. He took a small wire and cleaned the stem, then filled the pipe with fresh tobacco and lit it. No matter what he was doing, even cleaning his pipe, he was always thinking. You could see it on his face. Watching him light his pipe reminded me of Mr. McLeary trying to light his, just before he dropped it down the well.

Mr. Bell was taller and twice as wide as the young men. He couldn't stand close to the table like they did because his belly was too big. They leaned over the table when they wanted to touch something on the model. He just stood back and listened carefully as Mr. McCurdy explained why the flying machine needed such thin wings. It was the only way it could turn easily in the air, and it was easier to build. And they could make a whole bunch of them, he said excitedly, just like Henry Ford's automobiles or Thomas Edison's phonograph. When he said Thomas Edison, Mr. Bell frowned. "Or the telephone," Mr. McCurdy continued.

Mr. Bell raised just one eyebrow. He stared hard at the model but didn't say anything yet.

"It's similar to what the Wright brothers have on their plane," said Mr. McCurdy.

Mr. Bell took the pipe from his mouth. "Yes, but we haven't seen it fly." Then he looked at Mr. Baldwin. "What do you think, Casey?"

Mr. Baldwin shrugged his shoulders. "I don't know. I'd love to see it built full size. It's pretty slick."

Then Mr. Bell looked at me. "And what do you think, Eddie?"

I was so surprised that he asked me. I didn't know what to say. I wanted to agree with Mr. Bell, but Mr. McCurdy looked so hopeful that I wanted to agree with him, too. "I don't know, either. I guess I think that if I were up in the air in a machine, I'd like to know that I could come back down safely. But I think it looks pretty slick, too."

Mr. Bell had a big smile on his face. "Looks like it's two against two, Dougie."

Mr. McCurdy sighed. He reached over, picked up the model and brought it closer to Mr. Bell. With one hand he made the movement of the wind flowing toward the flying machine. "The air comes like this. It strikes the wings here, and the lift is quick and easy, like this." He raised the model up. "Then, when you want to turn, you just bank, like this, and around you come."

Now Mr. Bell looked more serious. "The tetrahedral cell, Dougie. That's the way to make the wings strong, yet keep them light."

Mr. McCurdy sighed again. This time, I got the feeling he was biting his tongue.

"The cell is too busy a design for flight, Sir," said Mr. Baldwin. "It's got terrific strength for any application on land, and endless possibilities, but it's cumbersome in the air, I think."

Mr. McCurdy nodded his head to agree. I was surprised to hear them disagree with Mr. Bell. I didn't think that anyone would. Mr. Bell raised his eyebrows again and looked at me, but I couldn't say anything because I didn't know what a tetrahedral cell was. So I shrugged.

"Looks like I'm outvoted," said Mr. Bell. He kept staring at the model.

"Let me build it," said Mr. McCurdy, "then you'll see."

Mr. Bell nodded. "Yes, yes, build it, of course. Let's see what it looks like."

Now Mr. McCurdy was smiling.

"You build it, Doug, and I'll fly it," said Mr. Baldwin.

Mr. McCurdy made a face just like one of my friends would. It was friendly, but it meant no. Mr. Bell moved to the other side of the laboratory, and I followed him.

He started to flip through some of his notepads, looking for something. It was getting dark outside the windows. It was time for me to go home. Mr. Bell tilted his head toward Mr. McCurdy, who was still standing beside the model with Mr. Baldwin. "Dougie first came here when he was a boy, Eddie, just like you. Look at him now. He's an inventor in his own right." Mr. Bell stared at me beneath his bushy white eyebrows.

"Tell me, Eddie. Have you decided which has been more useful to you, your successes or your failures?"

I was surprised that he remembered to ask me that. "Yes, Sir."

"And which would that be?" He squinted until his eyes were almost shut. I could tell that he really wanted to know. But how could I explain that I didn't really have any successes yet? The most successful I ever felt was standing here right now, in this room, with him and Casey Baldwin and Douglas McCurdy. But I wasn't going to say that.

"My failures."

"And why is that?"

"Because they make me work harder. And working harder makes me feel stronger." That was true.

Mr. Bell nodded thoughtfully. "Indeed." From the look on his face I figured he was going to say something serious.

"I must warn you about exceptions, Eddie."

"Exceptions?"

"To the rule. For every rule, we have exceptions. It's the darndest thing, but it seems to be part of nature, too.

Take the rule that Helen just shared with you: *i* before *e* except after *c*."

I didn't realize he had been listening the whole time. "Yes, Sir?"

"It's a good rule," he said. "It works most of the time. But how do you spell *eight*?"

I closed my eyes and concentrated. I wanted to spell it right. "*E-i-g-h-t*."

"Right you are! And so, which comes first, *i* or *e*?"

"*E*, Sir."

He took a puff from his pipe. The smoke made a cloud in front of his face. He squinted and looked through it at me to see if I understood. I nodded my head.

"The good thing about exceptions," he said, "is that they keep us on our guard. They keep us sharp. And that is surely a good thing." Then he winked. "Good day to you, dear lad." He slapped me on the back, turned and went back to the other men.

"Good day, Mr. Bell."

"Good day, Eddie," said Mr. Baldwin and Mr. McCurdy. They raised their heads, waved and dropped them again. They were anxious to keep discussing the model. I would be, too, if I were them. I wondered how long it would take Mr. McCurdy to build the real flying machine.

"Good day," I said, and went out the door. I closed it carefully. As I walked away, I could hear Mr. McCurdy's voice as he continued trying to convince Mr. Bell of the flat wings. I went to the end of the path, around the little cove and back across the beach. It was really dark now. I was late for supper.

Chapter 10

When I came home, my father was sitting at his desk. Once a week, he sat down and wrote letters to people far away. We had cousins in Halifax and Boston and distant relatives who lived in Scotland, though I had never met any of them. My father grew very serious when he prepared himself to write. He lit four candles, moved his books off his desk, sat up straight and just stared at the floor for a long time. No one ever interrupted him then, not even my mother. There was a special feeling in the house when he was writing to people far away.

When I came in, my mother hushed me to be quiet and pointed to a plate of food left on the table. With her eyes she questioned why I was late for dinner. I made a face to show I was sorry and mouthed the words, "I took a really long walk," which was true. I didn't want to tell her I had been to the Bells' house. Mouthing the words reminded me of speaking to Helen Keller. What an amazing day it had been.

My brother was sitting at the table, writing letters and trying to look like my father, even though he had nobody to write to. He looked up at me and raised his finger to his mouth to tell me to be quiet. I threw him a look that said "smarten up." He dropped his head and kept writing.

I knew that one day he would write as well as my father. Practice makes perfect.

Upstairs, my sister was lying in bed reading a book. She was always reading. She raised her head when I went past her door. "Where were you?"

"Nowhere."

"You were gone a long time."

"I know. I like to take long walks."

"Walking can't be *that* interesting."

"It is to me."

"You should read more."

"I will."

"When?"

"I don't know, I just will."

In my room, I sat on my bed, opened up the paper Helen Keller had given me and started to study it. There were fifteen words on the page. The last one was *tough*, and it was messier than the others because she had written it on her lap, standing up. I wondered if she had included it as a kind of joke, because learning was tough for both of us. She was definitely somebody who liked to joke and laugh and have fun. But she also probably worked harder than anybody else in the world. *She* was tough.

I stared at the words. They looked blurry to me, like the ridges of bark on an old chestnut tree. They were just shapes, like that. But when I stared longer and looked more closely, I saw the *g* and *h* in each of them. Since I knew that the last word was *tough,* I decided to learn it first. Now I saw that, strangely, there was no *f* in it. I said it out loud. Yes, there was definitely an *f* sound. Did she make a mistake?

I got up, went down the hall and poked my head into my sister's room. She didn't raise her head out of her book. "What do you want?"

"How do you spell *tough*?"

"*T-o-u-g-h.*" She spelled it and didn't even have to stop reading.

"Isn't there an *f* in it?"

"No."

"How come?"

"Because they didn't put one in."

"Then why do we say it that way?"

"Because that's how it sounds."

That didn't make any sense. I sighed. "Okay. Thank you."

"You're welcome."

I went back to my room and wrote out *tough* ten times. Then I looked for *fight*. I wanted to see if it had an *f*. Because it sounded like it did. Yes, it did. But the *g* and *h* in *fight* sounded different than they did in *tough*. In fact, they didn't sound at all. Maybe that was an exception to the rule. But what was the rule?

I went back to my sister's room.

"What now?"

"Is *tough* an exception to the rule?"

"What rule?"

"I don't know. Is it an exception to any rule?"

"No."

Now I was completely confused.

"Why are you still standing there?"

I took a deep breath. "Do you know why *fight* has an *f* and *tough* doesn't?"

She lifted her head out of her book, thought about it for a second then dropped her head again. "Nope."

"Then how are you supposed to remember?"

"I don't know. You just do. Do you remember how old you are?"

"Yes. But I can remember numbers. It's spelling I can't remember."

My sister looked at me, made a shrug with her face then dropped her head back into her book again. I returned to my room.

How were you supposed to remember how to spell words if there were no rules that you could trust or if there were exceptions to every rule, like Mr. Bell said? And how could you remember which one was the rule and which one was the exception? Wouldn't it be like trying to remember what every single leaf looked like on a tree? I wished somebody would agree with me that that was impossible. But nobody else seemed to care about it. Everybody else could spell.

I opened up my scribbler, wrote out the word *tough* ten more times, then *fight* ten times. I didn't know why *fight* wasn't just spelled *f-i-t*. Wouldn't that make more sense? If this were math, it would make more sense. That's what I liked about math. There were rules and no exceptions to the rules. I turned and stared at the window. If you had to learn to spell every single word by itself, then I was in big trouble, because I could never do that. And I didn't know how anybody else could. But they did. My sister did. My father did. My friends did. Even my brother was learning to. So why couldn't I? I looked down at the list that I had promised to learn, and I felt sick in my stomach.

The next day was Sunday and we had to go to church. I didn't mind going but hated having to dress up. I had one suit that used to be too big but now was too small. I had to wear it anyway. My wrists stuck out of the sleeves unless I pulled my shoulders up, which was uncomfortable if I did it for long. The pants didn't cover my socks and didn't even come close to my shoes. My mother said that I couldn't go to church unless I was dressed up, and I *had* to go to church. Once we were there, I folded my arms the way my father did, and that hid the shortness of my sleeves.

I was sitting there, between my mother and my brother, when all of a sudden somebody yelled out, "Where's the Pope?" Then there was laughter – something you never heard in church. Everyone turned around and saw Frankie MacIsaac standing up, until his mother and father pulled him back down in his seat. Frankie was twenty years old, but acted like a child. He had an accident on the farm when he was little, and now he would always be like a child. People said that he was simple. When I turned back in my seat, I saw my father staring at me. It made me uncomfortable. I wished I knew what he was thinking. Then when we were leaving, Frankie saw me and grabbed the arm of my jacket. "Hi, Eddie!" he said.

"Hi, Frankie."

"Hi, Eddie! Hi!" He seemed awfully anxious to talk to me. I glanced at my father. He was frowning and shaking his head at me. I turned away from Frankie and followed my father out the door.

That night, I had a disturbing dream. I was sitting on a fence along a road. Frankie was sitting beside me, and we were staring at the road where people were walking by. The people were all dressed up for church, but we weren't. I wanted to leave, but Frankie wanted to stay. "I think I'm going to go now, Frankie," I said.

"We should stay here, Eddie."

"No, I don't want to stay here, I want to go."

"But we can't go, Eddie."

"Why not?"

"Because we don't have any legs, Eddie! We don't have any legs!" And he started to laugh as if he were crazy. I looked down and saw that he was right, we didn't have any legs.

I woke to the sound of the back door slamming. It slammed so hard it shook the house. It must have been the wind. Then, I heard my father talking loudly with my mother. I wondered what was going on. I jumped up, got dressed and went down to the kitchen. My mother was sitting at the table with her arms folded. My mother didn't sit down very often. She looked upset. My father was standing in the doorway with a spade in his hand. When he saw me, he said, "Grab your jacket and boots."

"Yes, Sir."

"He hasn't had his breakfast yet, Donald."

"We won't be long."

My mother sighed heavily. "He needs to go to school."

My father looked at my mother, and his face softened a bit. He looked sorry. "He needs to learn skills that he can use, Mary. That's what he needs. He needs that more than school."

Chapter 11

I grabbed my jacket, pulled on my boots and followed my father out the door. My mother shoved a cookie into my hand. My father carried the spade and took long strides. I had to run to keep up. He never said a word to me all the way to the field. I ate the cookie quickly in case he did. The wind was blowing hard, and it was wet but not really raining yet. The field was on the back side of the hill, behind the house and on the other side of our best field, where the hill sloped down toward the woods. It wasn't deep, but it was wide. It was like a bald spot in the back of our farm. A useless piece of land. And that bothered my father.

The field rolled gently down to the woodlot, where the trees stuck up like a dark wall. The wind was pushing the first row of trees back and forth as if there were a giant stomping around in there. In spite of its being useless, I always liked this field. It seemed kind of hidden to me, like a secret. But it couldn't be plowed. The stones in it were too big. And they were too big to move.

I was surprised to see the horses there, standing side by side, attached to the plow. Their heads were dropped in the wind. I knew they wished they were in the barn. They didn't like storms. I was shocked to see that three or four rows of the field had been plowed. My father must have started in the middle of the night. Why was he trying to plow this field all of a sudden? At a glance, I could see that the rows weren't straight. He had worked his way around the stones. It must have been very hard. I followed him down to the horses. They turned and looked nervously at him. Then they rocked their heads when they saw me. They hoped I would take them to the barn.

I saw a crack on the blade of the plow. It had run straight into a stone, but you couldn't see the stone at all. My father held out the spade to me. "I want you to dig around it. I want to see exactly how big it is. I'll take the plow to the blacksmith, see if he can fix it."

"Yes, Sir." I looked at the horses. They were watching us nervously. "What about the horses?"

"The horses are fine."

My father unhooked the plow and wheeled it away. The wind wailed in the woods like a witch. The horses dropped their heads. My father yelled from halfway up the field. "Take the horses to the barn!"

"Yes, Sir!"

I stuck the spade into the ground, picked up the lead and pulled the horses around. They shook their necks and came gladly. I looked across the hill where my father was disappearing with the plow. The sun was coming up, but we would not see it today.

I returned the horses to the barn and gave them some feed. Three cats were sleeping in the corner of the stall. They raised their heads when we came in but didn't move. That told me the warm weather was over for sure. The horses didn't mind the cats, and the cats liked the heat of the stall in the winter.

Back outside, it started to rain. The wind blew it into my face and it stung a little. I dropped my head and returned to the field. I would have liked some breakfast but figured I'd better dig around the stone first, before my father came back. Even though the sun was up now, the field was still dark. The trees were swaying back and forth. The rain was coming down in sheets, and I was completely soaked. I picked up the spade and started to dig. I didn't know what skill I was supposed to learn that was new; I already knew how to dig. At least with the rain, the ground was soft.

The stone was less than a foot under the ground. I shovelled the earth away from the top of it and searched for its edges. Every time I thought I found an edge, I hit more of the stone a little deeper. It was enormous! I kept shovelling. My dream came back to me. What an awful feeling to have no legs. But why was Frankie in my dream? Where I removed earth, the rain washed the stone smooth, black and shiny. It sat in the ground like a gigantic black potato that had turned to stone. As the rain pounded on my back, I kept at it. Why did my father think it was okay for me to miss school? Did he think I couldn't learn? Did he think I was like Frankie MacIsaac?

I dug and dug without knowing how much time had passed. My belly growled. Then I saw a dark figure at the top of the hill. It came down the hill in the rain, carrying a basket. It was my mother. She was talking to me, but I couldn't hear her until she came close. "Where's your father?" Her face was twisted up in confusion at finding me by myself.

"He took the plow to the blacksmith. It has a crack in it."

"And left you alone to work in the rain?"

"He told me to shovel around this stone."

She looked down at the stone and frowned angrily. I think it was the angriest I had ever seen her. "Hurry up and finish so you can come home. You'll get sick if you stay out in this. Here. Eat this."

"Okay."

She handed me the basket but couldn't take her eyes away from the stone, as if it were some strange creature we had discovered in the ground. She shook her head. "This is a man's job. Eat quickly before the rain turns it to mush on you."

"Thank you."

She turned and went up the hill. I opened the basket and found a thick sandwich with butter and jam. There was a jar of milk, too. I turned my back to the rain and ate as quickly as I could and drank the milk. My hands were blistered, but it was probably the best milk and sandwich I had ever tasted. My mother had used lots of butter and jam. She wasn't famous like the Bells or Helen Keller, but she was just as nice. I liked that she had called this man's work. I dropped my head and got back to shovelling.

I didn't know how long I had been at it. With the rain falling and the wind howling, I just kept my eyes fixed on each side of the stone as I kicked the spade into the ground and pulled the mud away. Finally, I saw that I had worked my way completely around the stone. Now I was in a hole up to my waist, and the water was at my knees. The rain fell clean but turned to mud the second it landed in the hole. I climbed out, stood up and stared at the uncovered stone. It was as big as a cow! I turned to pick up the basket and saw my father's boots. He was standing right behind me. He scared me because I didn't know he was there. He wasn't looking at me; he was staring at the stone with a kind of frightened look on his face, as if we had found a monster. He narrowed his eyes, glared at the stone and spoke softly.

"Well, your mother was right. I must have been crazy to think I could plow this field. I may be master of this farm, but that stone is master of this field. That was decent work, Eddie. You can return to school now if you want to. Thank you." My father turned around and walked back toward the house. He didn't wait for me.

Chapter 12

I should have gone to school. But my father said I could return if I *wanted* to. That meant that I didn't *have* to. There was something else I wanted to do more.

Instead of returning to the house, I went into the barn. It was nice and dry. I went into the room where my father kept chains, rope and pulleys. There were several chains, three pulleys and lots of rope. I had never used the pulleys before, but had watched my father use them to lift heavy things in the barn. As I stood and stared at the equipment for a long time, I tried to form a plan in my mind. I wanted to move the stone all by myself but didn't know enough about it. I needed more information, and I figured I knew where to find it. But it would have to wait until tomorrow.

In the morning, I left for school before my brother and sister were ready. Miss Lawrence was sitting at her desk when I came in. "Good morning, Eddie. You're here early. What brings you to school early?"

"Hello, Miss Lawrence. I need to look up something in a book."

"Do you? Well, aren't you smart?" She didn't sound like she believed me. "And what book would that be?"

I looked up at the bookshelf. "That one. *Applied Mathematics*."

She looked up. "That one? That book is too hard, Eddie. You don't want that one."

"May I see it?"

"No. It's too…. Look, I'll show you." She went to the bookshelf, reached up and pulled the book down from the shelf. Balls of dust came with it. She handed it to me and then she sneezed.

I put the book down on a desk – it was really heavy! I opened it up, flipped through the pages and saw lots of pictures of people building things with blocks and triangles and carrying heavy weights on wheels and lifting things with ropes and pulleys. Miss Lawrence read the whole title out loud. "*Fundamentals of Applied Mathematics*. Eddie, I don't think this is the book you want to look at. I think you want to try something a whole lot simpler."

I kept flipping through the pages until I saw the pictures I was looking for. I didn't know how to spell *pulleys*, but I knew what they looked like.

"Eddie. I—"

"I found it!" I flipped through a few more pages.

"Eddie."

"I'm … just…."

"Eddie. This book is too old for you. Eddie?"

"Here it is. I found it, Miss Lawrence."

She looked at me with her disbelieving look.

"May I borrow this book, Miss Lawrence, just for a couple of days? I promise to bring it back."

"No, Eddie, this book is simply too difficult for you. I am sorry."

She picked up the book and started putting it back.

"It's for my father."

"For your father?"

"Yes."

"Oh. Well, why didn't you say so? Here you go. Don't forget to bring it back."

"I won't. Oh, and I can't come to school tomorrow. I have to help my father."

Miss Lawrence nodded her head, and now she wore her believing look. I felt a little guilty for not explaining everything, but I really *was* helping my father, and so I wasn't actually lying.

After school, I waited until my brother and sister left before I carried the book home. I took it to the barn and put it on a bench behind some rope. Then I went into the house, changed my clothes and sat down at the kitchen table for cookies and milk. My brother knew I was up to something and watched me closely and followed me out to the barn when I went to do my chores. But he got bored standing around watching me sweep and clean up after the horses. And I reminded him he was supposed to clean the chicken coop. Finally he left, and I could open the book in privacy. I might have shared my plan with him if he didn't keep correcting me all the time. It made me not want to be around him at all. I also didn't want him to tell anyone what I was planning to do.

I opened the book and found the pages with pictures of pulleys. There were arrows that pointed in the direction of a man pulling on a rope and a large box rising off the ground. There were pictures of simple pulleys and more complicated ones. The pictures were good at showing you how to set up the ropes. Then there were arrows in many different directions, and it was a little confusing. But the more I stared at the pictures, the better I understood. There were words too, but of course I couldn't make sense of the words. Did that matter? If the pictures showed me what to do, wasn't that enough? But I wasn't sure. Not knowing what the words meant made me a little nervous. What if they explained something really important that the pictures didn't show? I wished I could learn what the words said before I started.

After dinner, I tried to sneak the book up to my room, but my sister saw it. "What's that, an atlas?"

"No, it's a math book."

"It doesn't look like a math book; it's too big."

"It's applied math."

"You must be kidding."

"I'm not. I like math."

"Eddie, when I said you should read more, I meant *real* books, not math books."

"This *is* a real book."

"No, it isn't." My sister made a face and dropped her head into her book. I went to my room, lay on my bed and opened the book. On the top of the page, I saw the word *Archimedes*. What was that? I wanted to know, so I poked my head into my sister's room. "Do you know what *A-r-c-h-i-m-e-d-e-s* means?"

"I think it's a place."

"I don't think that's right. Do you have a dictionary?"

"I don't need a dictionary."

Then I remembered that my father had a dictionary. He kept it on the bookshelf with his other books – his prized possessions. No one ever touched his books but him. But maybe I could just borrow his dictionary for a couple of hours and be really careful with it, and nobody would notice. So I did. I went downstairs quietly, pulled the dictionary off the shelf, shoved it under my sweater and went back up to my room.

The nice thing about dictionaries was that everything was put in order with the alphabet, and it didn't matter how slow you were; if you were patient enough you could find whatever word you wanted. It took me a long time to find *Archimedes,* but there it was. "Archimedes. Ancient Greek mathematician. Born in 287 BC." Great. What did *that* mean? Well, I recognized the *math* part of *mathematician*. Then I looked up *ancient* and learned that it meant old. I knew that *BC* meant Before Christ, which meant it was a really long time ago. I stared at the word *born* and tried to say it. Suddenly, I knew what *Archimedes* was. It wasn't a thing, it was a person. It was the guy who had invented the laws for pulleys and other things. He was the guy that Miss Lawrence was reading about in school. Yay! I had figured it out. I went back to the math book and studied the pictures. Now I was happy.

I studied for a long time and had to look up more words in the dictionary, and that took forever and was exhausting, but by the time I went to sleep, I was pretty sure I understood how pulleys worked. For every pulley you added to a rope that was pulling something heavy, your work was cut in half. If you wanted to lift a stone that was twice as heavy, you had to run your rope through another pulley. You could lift something *really* heavy if you wanted to. In fact, you could probably lift a house off the ground if you used enough pulleys and rope that was strong enough.

But there were a couple of problems. First, every time you added a pulley, you had to use twice as much rope. Second, even though the pulleys turned on little wheels that made everything smooth, the more pulleys you used, the more friction there was against the rope. And that was dangerous. I had to look up the word *friction*. But even then I didn't understand it. That's what took me the longest. The pictures showed sharp lines coming from the pulleys and a danger sign and an arrow pointing to the word *friction*. But I was so tired when I looked it up, and frustrated and impatient. And I couldn't figure out what it meant. So I stuck my head into my sister's room and asked her what it meant. She took my arm and rubbed it really fast, until it got hot and sore and I had to pull it away. Then she looked up at me. "That's friction. Now go to bed."

Now I understood. If there was too much friction, or rubbing, the rope would get too hot and break.

If it weren't for the pictures, I wouldn't have understood any of it. But I did. And now I felt ready to try it. Except I needed more pulleys and rope. And the only place where I knew I could get more was down the hill, from Mr. McLeary.

Chapter 13

Studying books was way more work than digging around a stone in a field. I was so tired I fell asleep with my clothes on. And that's how I woke up in the morning. And I was late for school. My mother called up from the kitchen. "Hurry up, Eddie! You're late! Your brother and sister already left."

I climbed out of bed a bit confused because I wasn't completely awake yet. I came downstairs, washed my face and sat at the table for porridge. My mother looked at me with a worried face. "What's with you lately, Eddie? You've been acting strange."

"I have?"

"You have. It's not like you to sleep in. Yesterday, you went to school early. Today, you can't get out of bed. Hurry up and get going."

"Yes, Ma'am. Do you know where Dad is working today?"

"Your father is cutting firewood today. He won't be back until dark. Hurry up now. I've never seen you so slow."

"Yes, Ma'am." I gobbled up my porridge, grabbed my jacket and boots and went down the hill to the McLeary farm.

I found Mr. McLeary in his barn, walking behind the cow trough with a pail in his hand. He looked confused to see me there. He frowned with deep lines in his forehead, and his eyebrows went up, then came down, then went up again. "What are *you* doin' here?"

"Hello, Mr. McLeary. My father wants to know if he can borrow your rope and pulleys for just one day."

Mr. McLeary's eyes opened wide. "My rope and pulleys? Does he? Well, I don't see why not. I won't be using my rope and pulleys today. What does he need them for?"

I didn't want to tell him why I needed them. "He just needs them for one day. I'll bring them back tomorrow first thing."

He stared at me with his head tilted back, as if he were trying to stand up taller. He was already pretty tall. "I won't be using them today," he said. "Are you gonna carry them up the hill by yourself?"

I nodded my head. "Yes."

He started into a room at the front of the barn. I followed him in. "What did you say he needs them for?"

"Uh … he needs to make both sides equivalent." I knew from math that equivalent meant equal.

"He needs to make … oh, there you go, that's your father's fancy way of talkin'. What the heck does that mean?"

"I think it means both sides are supposed to be the same."

"Oh, that's right. I knew that. Yes, well, one of these days I might have to borrow your father's rope and pulleys and make both of my sides the same too."

"Okay."

Mr. McLeary handed me a large coil of rope, pulled three pulleys off the wall and dropped them by my feet. I bent down and tried to pick everything up, but it was too heavy and awkward.

"Here! Do it like this." He lifted the rope over my head so it would hang over one of my shoulders. It was heavy. "Here!" He handed me one pulley laid flat, then put the other two on top of it. "Carry them like that."

With my arms stretched all the way down I could just fit the three pulleys in my arms with my chin resting on top of the pile. It was a lot to carry, but at least it was balanced now. "Thank you, Mr. McLeary. I'll bring it all back tomorrow."

He nodded his head. "Tell your father I said hello."

"I will. Bye." I went out of the barn and started up the hill. I had to stop three times to rest. Without taking the pulleys out of my arms, I knelt down and rested with my hands on the ground, then got up again. When I reached the farm, I went around the yard and into the barn from the back door. It was so nice to put the pulleys down and peel the rope from around my neck. I took my father's rope, chains, pulleys and spade and piled everything into the wheelbarrow, then went out the back door and down to the rocky field. It was lucky my father would be away all day.

When I reached the stone, I saw that the hole I had dug all around it was completely filled in with water. That didn't surprise me. I went back to the barn for the horses and a bucket. I threw a harness on each horse and led them together out the back of the barn and down to the field. They were happy to come. It wasn't raining and the air was fresh and cool.

While the horses watched, I filled the bucket with muddy water dozens of times until the hole was empty. Next came the difficult part. I had to shovel a narrow tunnel underneath the stone so that I could pass a chain through. I needed to wrap the chains all around the stone so that they wouldn't come off when the horses started to pull. It was a lot of work and harder than I thought it would be, but eventually the two tunnels I dug from each side met at the middle. I shoved a chain in and pushed it through with the spade. Then I climbed down on the other side and pulled it up. Now I was covered in mud. That didn't matter; I was just so determined to make this work.

Once the chains were wrapped around the stone and linked together, I pushed the wheelbarrow over to the woods. This was the really tricky part. I had to choose five very strong trees where I could tie the pulleys. Each horse would pull one rope, and each rope would pass through three pulleys. But the two middle pulleys would be on the same tree. Between the pulleys, the ropes would make a shape like the letter *W*. One rope wouldn't be strong enough to pull the stone. It would break for sure. But two horses pulling two ropes through six pulleys should be strong enough. It was really strong rope.

It was lucky I had borrowed Mr. McLeary's rope because it was a long way to the first tree and I had to tie ropes together to make them long enough. I just hoped that the knots where I tied them wouldn't have to go through the pulleys, because they wouldn't fit.

I chose trees that were the same distance from the horses and the stone, on both sides, then tied the pulleys to them with chains and rope. When the pulleys were all in place, I went back to the stone and stared at the whole set up. It kind of scared me because the stone was so big and I was afraid that all I was going to do was break the ropes. Then I thought that maybe I could make it easier by shovelling the ground in front of the stone so that it would be like a ramp. Then the stone would slide out of the hole instead of having to be plucked out like a chestnut out of its shell. So I started digging again as fast as I could. Now I was really tired. But I wanted to make sure I was done before my sister and brother came home from school and told my mother I hadn't been there today.

Finally it was time to fit the ropes through the pulleys. I did the right side first. It took three pieces of rope tied together to reach the horses. Then I did the left side. It took only two pieces of Mr. McLeary's rope because it was longer. Then I moved the horses apart, tied two shorter ropes to their leads and tied the pulley ropes to the two harnesses on their backs. The field was wet, and the horses would have to pull uphill, but we were ready. I went back to the stone and took one last look. I wondered how long it had sat in this field. Probably millions of years. "Please work," I whispered, then went to the front of the horses, picked up the leads, pulled on them and called to the horses. "Come! Come! Come! Come!"

The field was wet and slippery but also rocky, and so the horses were able to grip the ground with their hooves. They were so strong. At first, they didn't move the rope at all; they just stepped sideways. They seemed surprised to find that they had to pull something so heavy. The second time I called them to come, they started to move up the hill, and they kept coming. I lowered my head so I could see beneath one of the horses, and I saw the stone rise out of the ground. It was like magic. "Come! Come! Come! Come!" I called again, and the horses continued up the hill. As they did, the stone slid down toward the woods. After about thirty feet, I stopped the horses, ran down to the pulleys and checked to see where the knots were in the rope. Then I had to run back to the horses and make them back up so I could untie the ropes and tie them again with the knots on the other side of the pulleys. Then I ran back to the horses and called them to pull again. I had to do that one more time before the horses pulled the stone to the edge of the woods.

I ran down the hill, untied everything, gathered it up and put it in the wheelbarrow. Then I went and took a good look at the stone in its new spot in front of the trees. Now it looked like a small dead whale out of water. I wasn't sure if it was ugly or beautiful. It would take some getting used to. My father had said that the stone was master of the field. I had to smile. No it wasn't. Archimedes was.

Chapter 14

I got back to the house just after my brother and sister came home from school. I had to bring the horses to the barn, go back to the field for the wheelbarrow and return Mr. McLeary's rope and pulleys. He wasn't in the barn, so I just hung everything up where it had been before. It was a lot easier to carry everything down the hill than it was to carry it up. But I was dead tired now and my shoulders were sore from the rope. When I stepped in the back door, my mother stood in the middle of the kitchen and stared at me. She looked me up and down. "You're full of mud. And your school clothes! And you weren't in school. Where were you?" She was angry.

I stared at the floor. "In the field."

"You were in the field?"

"Yes, Ma'am."

"What were you doing in the field?"

"Moving that stone."

She crossed her arms and stared hard at me, but her face looked more disappointed now than angry. "Eddie. Why didn't you go to school? Why would you spend the day out in the field trying to move a stone that can't be moved? Don't you want to learn? Don't you want to try? You can't give up." Her face softened. "My boy, you don't want to stop going to school."

"I'm not giving up. I just wanted to help Dad."

"Eddie, some things in life are just the way they are. You can't do anything about them. That stone is one of them. You just have to accept it."

"I moved it."

My mother looked even more disappointed now. She lowered her voice until it was almost a whisper. "Don't lie to me."

"I'm not lying!"

"You're lying," said my brother. My sister rolled her eyes and went upstairs. Now my mother was almost begging. "Eddie. Please don't lie to me. Your father said that that stone was impossible to move. I saw it myself. There is no way on earth you could move it by yourself."

"I did. I used the horses, and I borrowed rope and pulleys from Mr. McLeary."

"You're lying," said my brother.

My mother just stood and stared at me with her hand in front of her mouth. She was trying to make up her mind. "You did?"

"I did."

"You're ly—"

"Be quiet, Joey!" said my mother. She reached for her coat and scarf. "Okay then, show me."

My brother grabbed his jacket.

"No, Joey. You stay here," said my mother.

"But—"

"Stay here! We'll be right back."

I grabbed two cookies and followed my mother out the door. It was getting colder, and I was tired and hungry. I had missed lunch. I just wanted to eat a big meal, have a bath and climb into my warm bed. But I was excited, too.

We reached the top of the field and looked down at the woods. You could see the stone sitting there, looking very out of place. "I'll show you how I did it," I said, and started down the hill. But my mother stopped at the top and just stared with her hands on her hips. "No. I don't need to see how you did it. I can see it. That's enough." Then she threw me a strange look, but I had no idea what it meant. She turned around and started back toward the house. I hurried to keep up. "Can I have a bath?"

My mother laughed nervously. "Yes, my son, you can have a bath. I'd say you've earned a bath today." She turned and looked at me. "But tomorrow you'll go to school."

"Yes, I will. I promise."

After dinner, I was so tired that I went to bed early and fell asleep instantly. Some time after dark, I woke to find my father standing in my room, holding a candle. At first I thought I was dreaming, but I wasn't. When he saw me raise my head, he came over and sat on the side of the bed. He had never done that before. He started talking. But he sounded different, as if he were telling me a story. "I met Mr. McLeary today on my way home from the woods. He was coming from the blacksmith. He surprised me by asking me why I needed his rope and pulleys today. I asked him what he was talking about. Then he told me that you came and carried them home. I tell you, I was pretty angry at you then. Angry that you lied to him. Then I got to the house and was about to come up and shake you out of bed, but your mother told me that you had removed that stone from the field. Well, I didn't believe her. For fifteen years I've been married to your mother, and that's the very first time I didn't believe something she said. I had to see it for myself. So I did. I went out to the field. And I saw it. Under the light of the moon, I saw the big hole in the field, and I saw the stone sitting over by the trees. You just plucked that stone out of the field like it was a blueberry."

My father paused. He had never spoken to me for so long before. I didn't know what to say, so I just listened. He continued. "You did the work of three men today. Three men! You've got a mighty powerful will, my son." In the light of the candle I saw him nod his head up and down. "I learned something else today," he said. "I learned that you're smart. You're not just smart; you're as sharp as a razor. I had no idea before, but I know it now."

"I'm not smart in some ways."

"Well, everybody's not smart in some ways. I know that myself. But how did you know how to use the pulleys like that?"

"I looked it up in a book. It's called *Applied Mathematics*."

My father laughed. "You don't say. But how did you read it?"

"I didn't really read it. I just looked at the pictures. But I did look up some words in the dictionary." I just remembered I had forgotten to return his dictionary. "I borrowed your dictionary, Sir. I'm sorry I forgot to return it."

My father was quiet for awhile. I wondered what he was thinking. "Well, from now on, I would appreciate it if you would return my dictionary after you have used it. Do we understand each other?"

"Yes, Sir. I will. Thank you."

"Good then. You'd better get some sleep. You've got school in the morning."

"Yes, Sir."

He went to the door then stopped. "Eddie?"

"Yes, Sir?"

"Mr. McLeary said that he intends to make his sides the same now, too. What the heck is he talking about?"

"I don't know. I think he got mixed up about something."

"Yeah, I figured as much. Okay. Goodnight, my son."

"Goodnight, Sir."

I rolled over and felt a wave of happiness rush through me. This time I believed it would last.

Chapter 15

Over the fall, my father and I removed stones from the field. None of them was as big as the first one, but some were close. We only worked in the field on Saturdays, when I was out of school and my father could spare the time from other things he had to do. There were a lot of smaller stones that we just collected in the wheelbarrow. It was a long-term project. We had to stop when the ground started to freeze and planned to continue in the spring. My father did not expect to plow the field until the next fall.

This was a special time for me. I really enjoyed working with my father. It made me feel closer to him, even though we didn't talk much.

Things went very differently in school. We started learning to write essays. We only had to write one page, but that was pretty much impossible for me. Some of the other students thought it was fun, especially the girls, and they couldn't wait to show off their essays. Miss Lawrence told us to try to think of something we would like to write about, jot down some ideas, then try to form our ideas into sentences. Afterward, we would collect our sentences into paragraphs. Three paragraphs would make an essay. That didn't sound so hard to anybody else, but, really, I might as well have tried to fly to the moon.

First, I couldn't think of what to write about, and I just sat there, staring out the window while the other students were busy working. Eventually I decided to write about Helen Keller. So I tried to jot down ideas. But I didn't know how to spell the words. And I couldn't use the dictionary to look up the words because I didn't know how to spell the words in the first place. Because my topic was Helen Keller, and because I respected her so much, I tried my very hardest. I thought of words in my head and how they sounded, then did my best to write them down. By the time two of the girls had already finished their essays, all I had written down was six words: *def*, *blin*, *deturmint*, *brav*, *alon*, *intelajinz*. Miss Lawrence asked to see my work. I didn't want to show it to her. But she said that I had to let her see it, so I did. Some of my friends tried to look over her shoulder, but I told them to sit down, and I really meant it. I watched Miss Lawrence's face as she stared at my paper. She stared for a long time and looked confused, as if I had written a really long paper or something. Then she went to the bookshelf, took down the book I had borrowed before and carried it to my desk. She smiled like she was trying to be very nice. "Eddie. Why don't you look at this book while the other students write their essays?"

"Okay, Miss Lawrence." That suited me just fine. And that was the end of my attempt to write essays.

—

I hadn't seen Mr. Bell for a long time. One afternoon in the late fall, when I was out walking along the lake, I walked all the way to the woods of Beinn Bhreagh before I even realized I was there. I was so lost in a daydream. I was dreaming of a machine that was made of hundreds and hundreds of pulleys, with ropes spinning around and around inside of it. When the machine was attached to giant shovels, it could dig out mountains or dig deep trenches for canals in a single afternoon. If the machine was put on a large barge, it could raise sunken ships from the bottom of the sea. I wondered if Mr. Bell ever thought of a machine like that.

Since I was already so close, I thought maybe I would go up the lane to the Bell house and say hello. I hadn't been invited, but everyone there was so friendly, I was sure they wouldn't mind if I just stopped by to say hello.

But there was no one around when I climbed the steps of the porch. And it felt so different now. It was getting dark soon, and it was cold. I knocked on the door and waited a long time for a maid to answer it. It was the maid who had given me the cookie. She stuck her head outside nervously and told me that the Bells had gone to Washington, to their other home. I said thank you, turned around and walked away.

As I went back down the path, I passed the laboratory. It was closed up and dark inside. There was no one anywhere. Then, I noticed a small shed that had a light on inside it and smoke coming out of a pipe in the roof. I had never noticed this shed before, because I had always been staring at the laboratory. It was just a small shed. Maybe it was where one of the men who worked for Mr. Bell stayed. Maybe it was one of the men who looked after his sheep. Mr. Bell kept a lot of sheep. He bred them. He was trying to create a brand of "super sheep." I had heard that he drowned a sheep once and then brought it back to life with a special invention. I wondered if that was true.

I went to the door and stopped. I could smell tobacco smoke. Should I knock? But what would I say to one of the workers? And he wouldn't know me and would wonder what I was doing on the Bells' property. So I decided not to. I turned around and continued down the path. A few seconds later, I heard my name.

"Eddie?"

I turned around. There was Mr. Bell, standing in the doorway of the little shed, smoking his pipe. He made a wide sweeping movement with his arm. "Come on in, lad."

"Hello, Mr. Bell."

"I thought I heard a step outside," said Mr. Bell. "Though I didn't know if I actually heard it or imagined it. I think maybe I intuited it."

"What does that mean, Sir?"

"Intuition? It means I sensed you were there before I knew it. It's like having an inner knowledge." He smiled at me beneath his bushy eyebrows and pipe smoke.

"Your maid told me you had all gone to Washington, Sir."

He sucked on his pipe and looked apologetic. "Well, yes, we did. But then I came back. Mary is on strict orders not to tell anyone that I'm here."

"Oh." I wondered why.

"So I could be left alone and get some work done." Mr. Bell answered as if he had read my mind.

"I won't stay, Sir. I don't want—"

"No! Stay! Sit. It's nice to see you, Eddie. That's the irony of it – I complain bitterly for not having enough solitude to just sit and think. Then, the moment I've got lots of it, I start missing company. Here. Take a handful." He passed me a jar of candy. I opened the top and took two pieces out. It was hard maple candy. It was really good.

"Take more!"

"Thank you, Sir." I took one more. I was actually really hungry.

"What brings you out on this dark, chilly afternoon, my lad?" Mr. Bell opened a pot-bellied stove and shoved a piece of wood inside. The flames were already high. He shut the top with the hook and sat back down. He was wearing a heavy wool blanket across his legs. It was the same blanket I had seen his father wearing.

"I was just walking, Sir. And thinking."

He nodded as if agreeing with me. "And where did your thoughts take you today?"

The nice thing about Mr. Bell was that if he asked you something, it was because he really wanted to know. And he would take you seriously, no matter how simple your own thoughts might be. I told him about the machine I had been imagining. As I spoke, his eyes lit up, and he listened with great interest, so much so that I even wondered if he thought it might be a good idea. But when I finished, he pulled his pipe from his mouth and gave a stern criticism of the idea, just the way he had spoken to

Mr. McCurdy. But even though he pointed out its complete lack of being practical and forever removed the fantasy from my head in one quick stroke; the way he spoke to me, so seriously, made me feel very smart. I think maybe that was the smartest I had ever felt.

"It's brilliant. But it's a couple of hundred years too late. Once we harnessed steam, Eddie, we delegated pulleys to the barn and the pier. Now we're burning gas and oil. And I venture to say, before long, we'll have electric engines and solar-powered engines and wind engines and saltwater engines. The pulley is a mighty tool, but it's no match for the power we can generate with a single engine."

"Yes, Sir."

"It's a darn good idea, but it's two hundred years too late." He smoked thoughtfully. He was still thinking about it. I sat and sucked on one of the candies and stared at the stove. It was cosy in the little shed. It made me smile to think that this was the office of the smartest man in the world.

"And how goes the reading and writing battle?"

I almost blurted out, "Terrible! It's a complete failure!" But I caught myself. Mr. Bell wouldn't respect that. He was not someone who gave up. "It's a challenge, Sir."

"It's good to be challenged."

"Yes, Sir. Have you ever been challenged?" I couldn't imagine it.

He broke into such a big smile he couldn't keep his pipe in his mouth. He had to catch it with his hand. "The question should be, when have I *not* been challenged." He leaned forward, opened the little stove, tapped his pipe above it and emptied it. He closed the stove, sat back in his chair, reached for a wire on his desk and started cleaning his pipe. "A day doesn't go by that I don't wake to a challenge, my dear lad. If you were to measure a man's success by how many of his projects he has successfully completed, then you would have to consider me one of the worst failures the world has ever seen."

"But—"

"I can count my successes on these fingers." He held up his fingers. His pipe was stuck between them. "Those notebooks are *full* of my projects." He nodded toward a stack of notebooks on his desk. "And I've got more notebooks than I can count. All filled with projects." He leaned forward and started filling his pipe with fresh tobacco. "I'll be known as the inventor of the telephone long after I am gone. But Lord knows, nobody will ever know the wondrous inventions that have flown between these two ears. The telephone was just one of them. Albeit, a good one." He sat back, lit his pipe and stared at me as the smoke spread out from the end of it. For a few wonderful moments, we just sat in silence. I would remember those moments for the rest of my life.

Chapter 16

Every day, I carried the applied mathematics book home from school, lay on my bed and studied it, then brought it back in the morning. I wasn't learning how to write essays, but I sure was learning a lot about applied mathematics. Besides ropes and pulleys, there were triangles, arches, domes, levers, wedges, screws and ramps. A triangle was just a simple shape with three sides, but it was incredibly strong. In the book, there were pictures of famous temples, buildings and even bridges made out of triangles. Ever since ancient Greece, people have been building with them.

An arch was just a curved shape, like a bow when it was bent. The book showed pictures of bridges built with enormous arches. Some of the arches were made of stone, some of metal and some of wood. The metal and wooden ones were created with hundreds of small triangles. These were called *trestle* bridges. That was a word that I had to look up.

If you cut a hollow ball in two, the top half makes a dome. Domes were used for really big churches and important buildings. In the book, there was a picture of St.

Peter's Basilica in Rome and the Capitol in Washington. As fancy as these buildings were, they were created out of simple shapes that were discovered in ancient Greece. And that was applied mathematics. For me, that was the most interesting thing in the world.

Archimedes created tools out of levers, screws, wedges and ramps. If you put a really long screw, as thick as your arm, inside a tube, you could make a water pump. By pumping a lever at the top, you could spin the screw inside the tube, and water would get pulled up from the bottom to the top. This gave people the power to pull water out of the ground. A picture in the book showed people in the desert, their bodies and faces wrapped with cloth, feeding water to their camels from a pump.

Another picture showed men cutting down a giant tree with axes. The head of an axe was just a wedge with a really sharp edge. The handle was a lever. A wedge was really just a thin triangle on its side. So was an inclined plane. An inclined plane was a ramp. A ramp let you carry something uphill a little at a time instead of lifting it straight up. For fun, I bet three of my friends that I could lift them over my head all together. They laughed at me. Then I made them squeeze into the wheelbarrow together, and I pushed them up the hill until we were higher than we were before. They said that I cheated. I smiled and said that that's what the laws of applied mathematics let you do – cheat nature. Then they made faces at me and said that I was learning too much.

But to understand the book, the pictures weren't enough. I had to borrow my father's dictionary every night and look up words. I still wasn't reading; I was just looking up words and guessing. Then, one night, when I came down to get the dictionary, my father was writing letters. I didn't want to bother him, so I stood in the room and waited for him to say something. But he never did. So I quietly went to the bookshelf and pulled the book down. He never said a word. A little while later, I brought it back. He never raised his head. Later still, I was lying in bed, trying to sleep. But a word I had seen was bugging me. I kept seeing it, but couldn't figure out what it meant. I rolled over and over and told myself to forget about it. I would look it up tomorrow. But I couldn't. I couldn't sleep, because I kept trying to guess what the word meant. Finally I thought maybe my father was finished writing letters, so I snuck downstairs. He was still there! This time, he raised his head, looked over his glasses and frowned at me. "What do you want?"

"I'm sorry, Sir. I need to look up a word."

"Again?"

"I'm sorry."

"What's the word?"

I looked down at the piece of paper where I had copied out the word. "*R-e-n-a-i-s-s-a-n-c-e*."

My father pulled off his glasses, put his pen down, stood up and stretched his back like a cat. He reached for the dictionary and held it out toward me. "Keep it in your room," he said. I'll know where to find it when I need it."

I crossed the room and took it from him. "Thank you, Sir."

He just stared at me and nodded his head. He didn't like to talk when he was writing letters.

—

By the end of the fall, I had learned quite a bit about math, but had kind of given up trying to learn to write. I had looked up lots and lots of words and was getting faster at finding them in the dictionary. But when I did look up a word, it seemed to go out of my head just as fast as it went in. I didn't know why that was. Why couldn't I remember them? I didn't know how anyone could, there were so many! Math was easier because once you learned how to add and subtract numbers up to ten, you could add and subtract anything, with a little practice. But who could remember the rules of spelling and all the exceptions and how to spell the words in the first place?

But people did. Even the students in my school did. Some of the girls went around rhyming off the rules of spelling like it was a game. And we had spelling contests, and some of the girls never made a single mistake. I just sat and watched. The other kids in my school were all learning how to write essays. I had given up.

I didn't know what kind of job I would have when I grew up, but I knew it wouldn't have writing in it. I knew I could be a farmer if I wanted to, although I was pretty sure now that I didn't want to. I knew I would enjoy working with machines, and maybe I could do that without learning to write.

But I wasn't learning how to read, either, and that bothered me. I was just looking up words and guessing. And there had to be pictures. If there weren't pictures, I was lost.

But then something happened that changed my mind about giving up.

On the day we had our first real snowstorm of the season, my father had gone to town to buy some supplies and go to the post office. It was lightly snowing when he left, and the fields were still brown. By the time he came home, the fields, the house and the barn were covered in snow. Everything was white, even the sun.

My father came to the door, shook the snow from his clothes and banged his boots together before coming into the kitchen. He was red in the face and his eyebrows were wet with melting snow. But he just stood in front of everyone with a funny look on his face. "I went to mail some letters today," he said. "Then the postman asked me if I knew a Master Edward MacDonald. He said he couldn't think of who that was. He said it was important, too, because it was coming from Alexander Graham Bell, all the way from Washington. Well, it took me a minute or two to figure it out. But I did. 'That's my son,' I said." My father reached into his bag, handed me the package and shook his head with wonder. "It's for you, Eddie, from Alexander Graham Bell."

Chapter 17

The package was wrapped in soft brown paper and tied with white string. I carefully untied the string and unfolded the paper because I wanted to keep them. Inside I found a small book and a letter. The book had an orange cloth cover with a picture of a turtle and a warrior on it. My father said that it wasn't a turtle; it was a tortoise. The letters on the front of the book spelled Zeno's Paradox. I asked my father to read the letter out loud so that we could all hear it right away. He stood in the middle of the kitchen, held the letter out in front of him and read with his most serious voice.

My Dear Eddie,

I happened upon this small volume on a table in the Smithsonian Institute the other day and instantly thought of you. It seems to me there is nothing quite so fine as a good paradox to keep the mind as sharp as a chisel. Many is the day I have tramped through field and forest trying to solve this very riddle. Here, now, it is your turn.

Mr. McCurdy has built his flying machine. He will bring it to Baddeck in the winter and we will try it out on the ice. I hope you will come down to the lake to watch the flight.

Good luck to you with your writing, my young friend! Mrs. Bell and Miss Keller send their warmest regards.

Yours in friendship and the pursuit of learning,

Alexander G. Bell

No one said anything when my father finished. Everyone was thinking. My mother was smiling, and her eyes were wet. My father handed the letter back to me. "It's yours," he said. "You own it."

"Have you met Helen Keller, too?" asked my mother.

I nodded.

"And Mrs. Bell?"

I nodded again.

My mother's smile spread wider. I passed the book to everyone to let them look at it.

"Do you want me to read it to you?" said my sister.

I thought about it. "No, thanks. I'm going to read it by myself. I'll use the dictionary."

"That'll take a couple 'a years," said my brother under his breath.

"You mind your own business, Joseph!" said my father, and gave my brother a stern look.

"Yes, Sir." My brother dropped his head like a guilty dog.

I carried the book upstairs, lifted the dictionary off my desk and lay down on the bed. Before I began to read anything, I just explored the book inside and out. It was soft in my hands, like driftwood that had washed up on the lake. It was small and thin, and there weren't many pages, yet it felt like the nicest book in the world. Then I noticed a message written by hand inside the cover. "*For Eddie, a gifted young philosopher. Here's to a life of discovery! – Alexander G Bell.*" I had to look up the words *philosopher* and *discovery*, but I understood.

There were some pictures inside the book – old men with beards, like Mr. Bell, but they were dressed in clothing from thousands of years ago. There was a drawing of a horse and birds and fish. There was a drawing of a warrior and a tortoise, the same ones on the cover. It looked like they were racing. That was funny. Then there was a picture of another old man sitting on a step, deep in thought. Under the picture was the word *Zeno* and the dates, *490-430 BC.* I looked up *Zeno* and found out that he was a Greek philosopher. Even though I had already looked up the word *philosopher*, I had to do it again. It was someone who studied the meaning of life and a whole bunch of other things that I didn't bother looking up. I was pretty sure I knew what it meant; a philosopher was somebody who studied a lot. I didn't know why Mr. Bell had called me a philosopher. He must have been joking. What I needed to do next was look up the word *paradox*.

Well, I looked it up, but I didn't understand it at all. To understand the word *paradox*, I had to look up another word: *contradiction*. The dictionary said *contradiction* was a statement that made another statement not true. So I had to look up *statement*. A statement was just when you said something. If I said, "It's raining," that was a statement. Then, if my brother said, "No, it's not," he was making a contradiction to my statement. It took me a long time to understand that, but I finally did. But then, the dictionary said that a paradox was when a contradiction was also true. It was true and it wasn't true *at the same time*. That's the part I couldn't understand. How could something be true and not true at the same time? Then the dictionary gave an example – *Zeno's paradox*. Great. Now I was back where I started. And now I was too exhausted to do anything but go to sleep.

The next day was Saturday. It started snowing again in the afternoon. We weren't going to the field anymore, so after my chores I went up to my room, got cosy on my bed and opened the book. I spent the rest of the day in my room studying that little book, trying to figure out what the heck was going on. All I knew by the end of the day was that a warrior called Achilles was in a race with a tortoise, and it looked like the tortoise had won. But that didn't make any sense to me whatsoever, and I went to bed frustrated.

On Sunday, after church, I studied the book for the rest of the day but didn't get a whole lot further. Achilles was faster than the tortoise, but he couldn't beat him in a race. Why not? It just didn't make any sense. Before bed, I went to my father and asked him if he knew what a paradox was. He was sitting in his chair, reading a book. He raised his head, took off his glasses and stared at me. He said he wasn't sure, but he thought it was a riddle that was difficult to solve. I asked him if he had heard of Zeno's paradox before, and he said no. Then he asked me if I had started writing back to Mr. Bell yet. I was surprised. "Do I have to write him back?"

"Of course!"

"But … I don't know what to say."

My father put his glasses back on, dropped his head into his book and spoke without looking at me. "The smartest man in the world took the time to write you a letter, my son. I think you'd better get busy thinking of something to write back, don't you?"

"Yes, Sir."

The next day, I started writing a letter to Mr. Bell while the other students were writing essays. I didn't want anyone to know what I was doing so I opened the math book and put a sheet of paper inside it. I was trying so hard to think of what to say and to keep it a secret that I didn't even realize I had written *Deer Mr. Bell* with my left hand! It didn't look so bad, either. But I had used my left hand, just like Helen Keller. Then I noticed Miss Lawrence standing right behind me. "That's a good start, Eddie," she said, "but it's spelled *D-e-a-r*. A *d-e-e-r* is what runs in the woods. And you must use your right hand when you write, just like everyone else. Those are the rules."

"Okay, Miss Lawrence."

"Here!" She reached down, took the pencil out of my left hand and pushed it into my right. I didn't like that, and I didn't feel like writing anymore. But I remembered what my father had said – Mr. Bell had taken the time to write to me, shouldn't I take the time to write to him? And I wanted to, I just didn't know what to say. Then I thought of something. "Miss Lawrence?"

"Yes, Eddie?"

"Do you know what Zeno's paradox is?"

"Zeno's paradox? Well … a paradox is a kind of riddle, I think. But I don't think Zeno is a word. "

"Oh. Okay. Thank you, Miss Lawrence."

"You're welcome, Eddie."

I sat in my seat, stared out the window and thought. I knew that Zeno *was* a word. But Miss Lawrence didn't. That made me think that maybe she wasn't as smart as I had thought she was. And maybe, just maybe, she was wrong about using my left hand. If Mr. Bell had told me to use my right hand to write, then I would have trusted him and used it. If Helen Keller told me, I would have. They were both very smart and very nice, and I trusted them. But Helen Keller used her left hand herself. So why couldn't I? After thinking about it for a while, I decided to use my left hand when nobody was looking.

Chapter 18

In December, the School Inspector visited our class. He visited once a year. We always knew he was coming because Miss Lawrence would say, "Today, class, we'll have a special visitor." She always said it as if it was a good thing. But it wasn't. The Inspector was really boring and very bossy. But everyone treated him as if he were the king.

He came in the late morning, as he always did, and said all the same things he always said, although I wasn't really paying attention. I was staring out the window and daydreaming. After he finished talking, Miss Lawrence told us to get back to work. So I did. Then she and the Inspector had a conversation in whispers. A little while later, I was startled to see the Inspector standing right beside me, looking down at me with a fake smile on his face. He was holding a piece of twine. "Hello, Eddie MacDonald," he said.

"Hello, Mr. Inspector."

"Let me see your left hand." He said it like an order. I stuck out my left hand. "This is just the thing you need," he said. "This has cured plenty of left-handers, I promise you." He tied one end of the twine around my wrist tightly, pulled my left hand behind my back and tied the other end of the twine to the belt loop on the back of my pants. It was uncomfortable. I *really* didn't like it.

"There you go. Now, when you feel the urge to write with your left hand … you won't!" Then he slapped me on the back of my neck three times. It wasn't a pat, it was a slap. And it hurt. It made me angry. I felt like kicking him. I was also fighting back tears but didn't want anyone to see me cry. He had tied me up as if I were an animal. Then the bell rang. "Good day to you, children!" said the Inspector, and he went out the door.

I went outside with the other students for lunch break but could hardly hold myself back from crying. I started walking home. I didn't care if I was allowed to or not.

Jimmy Chisholm ran up to me. He had his jackknife in his hand. He cut the twine and freed my arm. "That was stupid," he said. "Just plain stupid."

I looked Jimmy in the eye and saw that he really felt bad for me. "Thank you, Jimmy," I said, and turned and went home.

My father was coming from the barn when I came up the hill. He smiled when he saw me. He didn't do that too often. Then he noticed that I had been upset, and he came closer to me. I wiped my eyes and tried to hide it from him, but he could tell that I had cried on my way home. I hated crying. It made me feel weak. I think I was just so tired from trying so hard to learn and not getting anywhere, even though I knew I had no right to complain when other people had it worse, like Helen Keller or Frankie MacIsaac.

"What's the matter?" my father said.

I shrugged. "Nothing, Sir. I'm fine."

"You're home at lunch. Tough morning at school?"

"I guess so." I shrugged again.

"Well, with a will like yours, you'll wear them down, Eddie. Don't let anybody stand in your way."

"No, Sir." I raised my hand to wipe my cheek, and my father noticed the twine tied around my wrist. He looked a little alarmed.

"What's that?"

"Um … a piece of twine."

"I know it's twine. What's it doing there?"

"The Inspector tied it there. He tied my hand behind my back."

"He *what*?" My father choked on his own words, and I never saw his face get so red so quickly before. "He tied your hand behind your back? And your teacher *let* him?"

"Yes, Sir."

"And why in Heaven's name did he tie you up?" My father was breathing heavily through his nose now.

"To keep me from using my left hand to write."

"Do you use your left hand to write?"

"I like to. It feels better. Helen Keller does it, too."

"Let me see your hand."

I raised my hand. My father squeezed his fingers underneath the twine and tore it off like it was nothing. "Turn around." I turned around and he ripped the twine from my belt loop. "Is your teacher still at school?"

"Yes, sir."

"Okay, Eddie. You go in and get yourself a bite to eat. I'll look after this." He put his hand on my chin and looked into my eyes. "It's not a perfect world, my son. There are all kinds of problems for everybody every day. That's just the way it is. But let me tell you something: don't ever let anybody lay a hand on you like that again. Nobody has the right to touch you without your permission. Do you understand me?"

"Yes, Sir."

"Good. And something else: use the hand that God gave you to use, and don't let anybody tell you any different. If God saw fit to make your left hand stronger than your right, then so be it. Who on earth can say different?"

"Yes, Sir."

"Okay then."

My father let go of my chin, took a deep breath and started down the hill toward the school. I watched him go. I was sure glad I wasn't Miss Lawrence right now. I wished I could have followed him down the hill and peeked through the window when he spoke to her, but I knew I'd better not.

The next day, Miss Lawrence was extra nice to me but seemed a little nervous. When I opened the math book and continued writing the letter to Mr. Bell, she smiled at me but never came over to look. She told me to ask her if I needed any help, but I got the feeling she was hoping I wouldn't ask. And I didn't.

It surprised me how much better my writing was with my left hand. My left hand was steadier and more confident. It didn't help me to spell, but it sure looked better when I was done.

It was still messier than the other students' work though, mostly because I kept making mistakes and having to erase them. Why were words not written the way they sounded? Why were some written the way they sounded and others not? Why couldn't they all be the same? Why was the word *hurry* spelled with a *u* and the word *worry* spelled with an *o* when they sounded exactly the same? And how were we supposed to remember that? It was crazy! I knew that we were supposed to memorize all the words in the English language, but it seemed to me that that was about the same as memorizing all the rocks on the beach, and that was impossible for anybody!

Still, I knew that the other kids in my school were learning how to spell all the words and learning how to read and write, and I wasn't. Maybe I could have accepted that, maybe, but I really wanted to write back to Mr. Bell, especially since I had finally figured out Zeno's paradox, and I wanted to tell him that.

Chapter 19

I tried to explain Zeno's paradox to my mother first, but she couldn't understand it, and she got frustrated and finally asked me to stop talking. Then I tried my sister, but she couldn't get it and said that I was making it all up and that it was just silly. I asked Miss Lawrence if she wanted to hear it, but she just smiled at me and said, "No, thank you, but I'm sure it is just wonderful."

So I tried my father. I waited until he had finished his supper and was sitting in his chair, smoking his pipe. I came into the room, cleared my throat and waited until he looked at me.

"Yes?"

"Excuse me, Sir. Do you think I could explain Zeno's paradox to you to see if I am making any sense?"

"You want to explain it to me?"

"I want to write in my letter to Mr. Bell that I understand it. I think I do, I just want to make sure."

My father held his pipe with one hand, folded his arms and smiled. "Go ahead."

"Okay. It goes like this. Achilles was a great warrior. And he could run faster than anybody else. Then one day, he raced against a tortoise. The tortoise was slow, but it always went the same speed. Achilles was so sure he would win the race that he gave the tortoise a head start. When the tortoise was halfway to the finish line, Achilles started running. When he got to the halfway point, the tortoise had moved only a short distance. So Achilles ran that short distance. But when he got there, the tortoise had moved a shorter distance. It was very short, but even so, the tortoise had moved. So Achilles ran that shorter distance. But when he got there, the tortoise had moved again, a tiny distance. When Achilles ran that tiny distance, the tortoise had gone further. And so, no matter how many times Achilles chased after the tortoise, he could never catch him because the tortoise was always moving and Achilles was always catching up. So the tortoise won the race, even though Achilles was faster. And that's why it's a paradox, because both things can't be true, but they are."

I stopped and waited for my father to say something. He had listened very closely and was nodding his head. "Yup. I get it. I mean, I think I get it. Steady wins the race. Isn't that the darndest thing? It doesn't make sense, but it does. And that's what you call a paradox, is it?"

"Yes, Sir."

My father sat back in his chair, took a deep puff from his pipe and let the smoke out. He almost looked like Mr. Bell behind the smoke. "Maybe … maybe before you send that letter, you might want me to take a look at it, would you?"

"That would be great! Thank you."

"Okay then."

I turned to go.

"Eddie?"

"Yes, Sir?"

"I don't think you're cut out to be just a farmer. I think you're meant for something more than that."

I smiled. I thought so, too.

—

I never worked so hard in all my life as I worked on that letter to Mr. Bell. It was only two pages, double-spaced, but I worked on it every day at school and every night for the rest of the term. Then, when school ended for the Christmas holiday, I kept at it every day. I wrote the letter out seven times, and three times I brought it to my father, and he corrected it for me. But then, the day I finished it, something terrible happened. I discovered that I had lost the book Mr. Bell had given me.

I didn't know how it could have happened. I had kept it with me all the time and was so careful with it. My mother helped me search the house from top to bottom, but we never found it. The only thing I could think was that I must have dropped it on my way home from school, and it got covered in snow. I went out and spent a whole day raking the snow all the way down the hill but never found it. That made me very sad. My mother said that maybe it would show up in the spring. Well, it might, but what would it look like then?

And then, on Christmas Eve, I got it back in the strangest way.

My mother sent me down to the McLearys' with a sugar pie for Christmas. I carried the pie all the way down the hill through the snow and walked across the porch and knocked on the door. Mrs. McLeary came to the door and greeted me. "Well, if it isn't the neighbours! And if it isn't the neighbours carrying a sweet-smelling pie!" Mrs. McLeary lifted the pie out of my arms. "Won't you be a dear, Eddie, and run into the barn and tell Mr. McLeary to come to the house?"

"Yes, Mrs. McLeary."

I went to the barn. All of Mr. McLeary's cows were inside the barn, and it was nice and warm. But I didn't see Mr. McLeary. I looked everywhere, but he wasn't there. Then I thought I heard him sighing up in the hayloft. I climbed the ladder and looked. There he was. He was sitting on a bale of hay, with a lantern, and he was staring at something in his hands. It was my book!

"Hello, Mr. McLeary!" I called. "Merry Christmas!"

"Huh? What? Oh. Merry Christmas. What are *you* doing here?"

"Mrs. McLeary told me to tell you to come to the house."

"She did, did she? Okay. All right then. I'll do that then." He dropped his head into the book again and didn't move. I didn't know what to do or say. I took a deep breath. "Um … that's my book."

Mr. McLeary raised his head and stared over at me. He just stared with a tired and kind of sad look. I waited for him to speak. "It's your book, is it?"

"Yes."

He looked down at the book again. Then he looked back at me. "Will you read it to me?"

It was probably the strangest thing I ever did, but I sat on the hay and told Mr. McLeary the story of Zeno's paradox. I didn't read it to him; I just told it to him, but I made it sound like a story, and I didn't think he knew the difference. If he did, he didn't say anything. He listened very carefully to every word, and when I was finished, he asked me to read it again, quickly, before he had to go into the house. So I did. When I finished, he stood up, raised his head high and pulled on his suspenders. "My, that's a great story! Isn't it somethin' what you can find inside a little book like that? I never had anybody read me a story before."

"Really? Never?"

He shook his head. "Nope. But you made that little book come alive. It's just like magic, isn't it?"

"Yeah, I guess so."

Mr. McLeary smiled and frowned at the same time. We climbed down from the loft. At the barn door, he pulled on his coat and cap and looked down his nose at me. His eyes were shiny. "What I wouldn't give to have a brain like yours," he said. Then he lifted his cap. "Merry Christmas to you, young Eddie."

"Merry Christmas, Mr. McLeary."

I wandered slowly back up the hill. The snow fell on my face and melted. It was one of those times when it would snow all night, I could just tell. In the morning, everything would be hidden under blankets of white. I loved it when it snowed on Christmas Day.

My mother was standing over a pot on the stove when I came in. She loved it when it snowed like this, too. She threw me a happy look while I hung up my jacket and pulled off my boots. I bet she smiled a lot at Christmas when she was a girl.

"You found your book?"

"Mr. McLeary had it."

"He did? Did he find it?"

"Yes. I think he wanted to keep it."

"Well, I can understand that; it's a pretty book."

I pulled off my socks, hung them behind the stove to dry, came around the stove and stood beside my mother in my bare feet. I stared into the pot she was stirring. The house was filled with the smell of mincemeat. "Did you know that Mr. McLeary can't read?"

"He can't? Well, that doesn't surprise me. Lots of people can't read. We aren't born knowing how to read, you know." My mother grinned. She was in a really good mood. "It's not like with birds, born knowing how to fly."

I thought about that while I watched her stir the mincemeat. "Most people would rather fly than read," I said, without taking my eyes from the pot. The spices in the mincemeat were tickling my nose.

"Oh, I don't know; I bet if you asked all the people in the world whether they'd rather learn to fly or learn to read, I bet most of them would choose to read."

"I wouldn't. I'd choose to fly."

My mother dipped a wooden spoon into the mincemeat, pulled it out and gave it to me. She looked serious for a second, then went back to smiling. "Maybe that's the problem, Eddie."

I thought about it while I licked the spoon. No, that wasn't the problem. I knew I wanted to learn to read, but reading would always be a struggle for me. Birds made flying look effortless.

Chapter 20

It was crowded in church on Christmas Day. I didn't mind going to church on Christmas, because the church was decorated, smelled nice and there was a special energy in the air. Everyone wore so much clothing and squeezed into the pews so tightly, it was toasty warm, which was a lot better than sitting in a cold church. And even though the mass was longer on Christmas, and I had to fight to stay awake, I didn't mind. Afterwards, there was a reception with cookies, cakes and sweet drinks. Everyone stood around smiling, chatting and having a bite of something sweet.

Usually I stood with my mother, brother and sister, while my father stood with the men and talked. Just for a while. Then we all went home together. But this year, for the very first time, my father tugged on my coat sleeve and pulled me along with him. My brother tried to follow, but my father told him to stay. I raised my head and smiled at my brother, and he made a face at me like a pig.

As we approached the other men, I heard a man say Mr. Bell's name, and my ears perked up.

"They're gonna fly it over the ice," said the man. The other men's eyebrows were raised as if he had said they were going to fly it to the moon.

"Well, *he's* not gonna fly it, Joe. It's the young McCurdy who'll fly it. Bell doesn't do the flying; he just does the thinking."

The other men laughed.

"It'll never get into the air," said another man. He sounded like he really knew what he was talking about. I wondered if he did.

"Not in the cold anyway," said a third.

"Cold's got nothin' to do with it. It's not a kite, Bill. We're talking an engine here and a whole lot 'a weight, not to mention a man on board. It's going to carry a man, you know."

The first man shook his head. "Ah, I can't see it happening. I can't see it getting off the ground. Look what happened when they flew that big kite this time last year. Did you see it?"

"I saw it. Big as a barn."

The other men nodded their heads.

"It crashed."

"The bigger you build it, the harder it'll fall."

The men laughed again. My father didn't.

"Nearly killed a man," said one of them.

"I dunno. Seems to me the man's inventing days are behind him, don't you think? Seems like a heck of a lot of expensive experiments for nothing. I mean, it's his money. It's his business."

"If we were meant to fly, don't you think we would have been given wings?" said the first man. "What do you think, Donald?"

All the other men turned to look at my father. My father took the pipe from his mouth, stared at the ground and thought for a second. The other men waited. "I honestly don't know. But I'll tell you one thing: I'll be out on the ice to watch."

"Me too."

"Yes, I wouldn't miss that."

"That's for sure."

On the way home, I walked close to my father. We went quietly for awhile, but I was wishing he would say something. Finally I couldn't keep it to myself any longer. "I think it will fly," I said.

My father didn't answer right away. He was staring across the snowy fields. Then he said something that I never expected to hear him say. "Wouldn't it be something though? I always dreamt of flying, myself."

"Really?"

He nodded but didn't say anything more. He didn't speak again on the way home. He just stared across the fields. I kept wondering what he was thinking. When we came into the house and pulled off all our winter clothes and hung them up, and my mother and sister got busy with our Christmas dinner, I couldn't help but ask my father one more question. It was bugging me too much. "Do you think Mr. Bell's inventing days are behind him, Sir?"

My father stood in the kitchen and stared at me. I knew he was wanting to go into the parlour, sit in his chair with his pipe, read the paper and be left alone. Talking with people once a week in church was more than enough company for him. But he answered me just as thoughtfully as he had answered the men at church. "I wouldn't think so, Eddie. There's no reason to think that inventing is a young man's game. Seems to me a man might grow smarter as he grows older, if he keeps his mind sharp. Of course, I've never met the man. But you have. I figure you'd be a better judge of that than me." He paused. "Your letter is done, is it?"

"Yes, Sir." I liked his answer.

"Bring it to me then. I'll address an envelope for you, and we'll mail it first day the post is open."

"Okay. Thank you, Sir."

I went upstairs to get the letter. As I passed my sister's room, I saw her holding a doll that she had dressed in silk clothes she had made herself. The silk had come from Mr. Bell's giant kite that crashed the year before. It had been made with thousands of squares of fine red silk. When it smashed, the silk floated to the beach, where people picked it up and took it home. My sister made doll dresses out of it.

I stared at the doll. For a second, I wondered if maybe the man at church had been right. Was Mr. Bell too old now? Was he just making expensive mistakes? But then I had another thought: who would I rather trust, Mr. Bell or the men at church? That was easy.

In my room, I looked over the letter. As I stared at the words scratched onto the paper with a pencil, I thought of how much harder it had been to create than it had been to pull the stones from the field. It didn't look like it should be so hard, but it was. It didn't surprise me that so many people never learned to read and write, like Mr. McLeary. What was amazing to me was that so many people did.

While snow slowly covered the window from the outside, I read my letter for the last time.

Dear Mr. Bell,

Thank you for sending me a letter and a book. It was the first time I ever received a package in the mail. The book is wonderful. At first, it was too hard to understand Zeno's paradox, but now I understand it. I also learned more about Archimedes and his laws of applied mathematics.

We used pulleys to remove big stones from our field.

We are all very excited that you and Mr. McCurdy are bringing a flying machine back to Baddeck.

We will come down to the lake to watch it fly. Some people say it won't fly, but I know that it will. I wish that Helen Keller could see it fly, too. I still find it hard to read and write, but I will never give up. I wrote this letter out seven times. My father helped me. It is cold here now and the fields are all covered with snow. Thank you again for writing to me and sending me such a wonderful book. It is my favourite thing.

Yours truly,
Eddie MacDonald

My writing wasn't smooth and flowing like my father's writing. It wasn't tall and straight like Helen Keller's writing. It was somewhere in between. Part of me couldn't believe that I had written it at all. But I had. I brought it downstairs and handed it to my father.

"Thank you," he said. And that was all that he said.

For Christmas dinner we had turkey, potatoes, dumplings, carrots, turnip, beets, radishes, peas, stuffing, cranberry sauce, bread and gravy. For dessert we had apple and mincemeat and sugar pies. I ate until my belly was full, and then I ate until it was sore. I crawled upstairs, fell on my bed and listened to the snow tapping on the window like grasshoppers. The words of my letter drifted through my head. I could see each word clearly. I had memorized them all without even trying to because I had worked so hard on them. It really was like memorizing the shape of every leaf on a tree. But it was just one little tree. There was a whole gigantic forest around it.

Chapter 21

Now it was January 1909. Everyone was saying that the world was going to change so much we wouldn't even recognize it anymore. It seemed to me they said that every year. But now, automobiles were going to be everywhere because the Ford Motor Company was making one that everybody could afford. It was called the Model T. There would be so many of them on the roads we wouldn't even need horses anymore. I found that kind of hard to believe. Where would all the horses go? When I asked my father if we could afford a Model T automobile, he just laughed. "Don't believe everything you read in the newspapers," he said.

Well, I never read it; I just heard it.

In school, everything was pretty much the same. We started learning fractions in math. Some of the older students knew them already, but most of us were learning them for the first time. While Miss Lawrence explained what a fraction was, I stared at the pictures in the book, because that was the easiest way for me to learn. One picture showed a pie cut in six pieces. Another picture showed two pieces of the pie, and beside it was the fraction 2/6. Another picture showed four pieces, and the fraction 4/6. That looked pretty simple. If you added the two pieces to the four pieces, you got six pieces, which was the whole pie. In fractions, that meant: 2/6 + 4/6 = 6/6, and that seemed pretty clear to me. And that's all that fractions were.

It got more complicated a few days later when we had to add fractions that had different bottom numbers, like 2/6 + 3/7. I struggled with that for a while, but eventually I got it. And I was the first one who did. Then we learned how to multiply fractions. I found that even easier. For me, math was like a puzzle that you had to figure out, like Zeno's paradox. It was almost a kind of game. And it had rules that stayed the same and weren't full of exceptions. It made sense to me.

But it didn't make a lot of sense to some of my friends. And it didn't make *any* sense at all to Jimmy Chisholm. I saw him wrestling with it in his head, and his eyes went up and down a lot, and his face got redder and redder, and he started to puff out his cheeks as if he was going to blow up. I saw him write the numbers down in his scribbler then erase them. He wrote them again then erased them again. Then he stared out the window and looked like he wished he was somewhere else. Boy, I knew that feeling. Finally Miss Lawrence told me to go and sit beside Jimmy and help him with his fractions. So I did.

After math, we had reading. I went from helping somebody else and feeling smart to not even participating. Miss Lawrence always left me alone to do my own work now. I could use my left hand if I wanted to, and I could look at whatever I wanted. She didn't care. And now that she wasn't reading about ancient Greece anymore but something really boring, I stopped paying attention when she was reading out loud.

But I *was* learning to read and write something, sort of. Every day, I opened up *Zeno's Paradox* and read the first few sentences. "Zeno was a philosopher in ancient Greece…." I wasn't actually reading though, I was just learning the words and memorizing them. I would say them in my head over and over and write them down. And every day I added at least one more sentence. At least I felt I was doing something like the other students. And I *was* learning, even though it was terribly, terribly slow. Maybe it would always be that slow, I didn't know. But I wouldn't stop. Helen Keller would always be blind and deaf, and that wouldn't stop her. So why should I stop? I wouldn't.

—

I knew that Mr. Bell was coming back in the winter. And Douglas McCurdy was bringing his flying machine and was planning to fly it over the lake. The flying machine was called the *Silver Dart*. Mr. Bell had already invited me to come and watch. And I wouldn't miss that for the world. But January passed and no one came. What a long month it was! Day after day, I waited for news of their return, but they never came. And every day in school I studied fractions and memorized the little book until I could read the whole first chapter from memory. And every day I stared out the window and wondered when the *Silver Dart* would come to Baddeck. It was starting to feel like it never would.

Then one morning near the end of February, in the dead of winter, when everything was frozen and it was even too cold to snow, Miss Lawrence told us that we were going to have a special visitor. I thought, "Rats, the Inspector is coming *again*?" He wasn't supposed to come so soon. Sure enough, in the middle of the morning, there was a knock on the door. Miss Lawrence's face turned beet red. She started fixing her hair, straightening her dress and she raised her finger to her mouth to signal for us to be silent. And we were. She went to the door, opened it and in stepped Mr. Bell.

His face looked redder and his hair whiter than last I had seen him. He also looked taller and rounder. He took off his cap, nodded to Miss Lawrence and shook her hand. Standing next to him, Miss Lawrence looked really small.

"Class," said Miss Lawrence. She was a little nervous. "We have a very special visitor today. This is Mr. Alexander Graham Bell."

Mr. Bell took out a handkerchief, blew his nose and said, "Good morning, class!"

Nobody said anything. Everyone just stared until Miss Lawrence said, "Class?"

"Good morning, Mr. Bell."

"I think I have a friend in this class," said Mr. Bell, and he stared over the heads of the students until he saw me. He winked at me. "Yes, there he is. Eddie! Come up and say hello."

I climbed out of my seat with my book and went to the front of the class. Mr. Bell held out his hand. "Hello, my dear friend. I see you've got the book I sent you."

"Yes, Sir." I shook Mr. Bell's hand. He patted my shoulder with his other hand. I knew my friends were staring at me, but I didn't look at them.

"How is the reading and writing coming along? You certainly sent me a good letter. Have you been reading this book?"

I took a deep breath. "Yes, Sir. It hasn't been going too badly. But it's a lot of work."

He smiled and nodded. "Yes, yes, of course it is. But you're doing it."

"Yes, Sir. I memorized the first chapter."

Mr. Bell raised his eyebrows and stood up straighter. He was really surprised. "You did?"

"Yes, Sir."

"Well, I don't know about the rest of you, but I sure would like to hear that. Will you read it to us, Eddie?"

I looked at Miss Lawrence. Her face was still red. She smiled awkwardly and nodded her head.

"Okay." And so I did. The first chapter was only four pages, so it didn't take too long. Since I knew it by memory, I didn't have to look at the words. But I did anyway, so that it looked like I was reading. Maybe you could say that I *was* reading, in a way. But if everyone worked this hard to read, it really would take a couple of years to get through a whole book. I guess my brother was right about that.

When I finished, Mr. Bell clapped. Then everyone else clapped. Miss Lawrence clapped too, though she had a confused look on her face. She looked surprised that I had read so well, but maybe a little angry because she probably thought I had been pretending I couldn't read. I would try to explain it to her later.

"That was marvellous, my boy! Marvellous!" Mr. Bell looked at the class. "Wasn't that splendid?"

Everyone clapped again. Then Mr. Bell said that they would be flying the *Silver Dart* on the lake next Tuesday, and he invited everyone to come down and watch. He thanked Miss Lawrence for the welcome, said goodbye to the class, patted me on the back, winked and went out. I went back to my seat. I felt about ten feet tall.

Chapter 22

Everyone in Baddeck was planning to go down to the lake, step out on the ice and watch, even though many people didn't believe the *Silver Dart* would really fly. Miss Lawrence cancelled school for the day so that all the kids could go. I was so excited. I was especially happy that my father would finally meet Mr. Bell. He joked that he was the only man in Baddeck who hadn't met Mr. Bell yet. He had seen him from a distance several times but had never actually met him up close or shaken hands with him. One way or another something had always come up that prevented him from having the opportunity. Well, not *this* time.

The *Silver Dart* was supposed to fly in the afternoon, but people already started gathering on the ice in the late morning. My father went out to the woods early to cut some trees. He said he'd be back by lunchtime and we could all go down to the lake together then. He said that ought to be plenty of time. My father liked to be early but didn't want to stand around all day waiting to see something that might not even happen. Even though he believed Mr. Bell was the smartest man in the world, he said he would have to see a machine carry a man into the air before he would truly believe it. My father remembered when the gigantic kite had smashed. He never saw the flight but went down to the lake the next day and saw the pieces wash up on shore. A lot of people thought that Mr. Bell was trying to do the impossible.

My mother spent the morning making a picnic that we could eat on the ice. We got our warmest clothes out and put blankets and furs in the small sled. We would walk down through the snow and pull the sled behind us. My brother and sister and I would bring our skates.

But by lunchtime, my father hadn't returned. We waited and waited, until my mother got impatient. "Oh, well, isn't that just like your father – he complains he hasn't met Mr. Bell, and then he doesn't show up when he has the chance. Oh, that man!"

We waited a little longer. We were all dressed now and sitting in the kitchen, sweating. Everyone was quiet, and you could hear the clock tick as if there was no one in the house.

"Okay, that's enough!" said my mother. "Let's go. Your father can catch up when he gets back. If we don't go now, we'll miss the whole thing." It surprised me to see my mother so excited.

So we went outside and started down the hill. My brother and I pulled the sled, and my mother and sister walked in front. I kept looking back to see if my father was coming, but he wasn't. When we got to the bottom of the first hill, a light wind on the top of the hill blew dry snow across the field, and you couldn't see the house anymore. It bothered me that my father was not with us.

I felt like we were abandoning him. As much as I wanted to get to the ice and see all the excitement, I didn't want to go without him. So I stopped.

"I'm going to go back and look for Dad," I said.

My mother stopped and turned around. "He might not come. You know your father."

"I know, but he's probably just on his way. And then we can catch up with you."

My mother looked at me sternly. "Eddie. You will miss the first flight of a flying machine in the whole British Empire."

I knew then that my mother really believed it was going to happen. This was a difference between my mother and father – my father had to see something to believe it. My mother didn't.

"We won't miss it," I said. "We'll catch up." And I really believed that.

"Emily. Help Joey pull the sled," said my mother.

I started back. "I'll follow the horses' tracks into the woods," I said. "We won't miss it."

My mother frowned, turned around and kept going. My brother and sister followed her. I went up the hill as quickly as I could. Now I was worried we were going to miss the flight.

The horses' tracks were easy to see. The sky was clear and the shadows in the snow were bright blue. The tracks of the sled made two blue lines that disappeared into the woods. I was glad the snow was crunchy and held my weight. If I were sinking with every step, it would have taken forever to get through the woods, and I would have been exhausted.

As I approached the woods, I saw the stones we had cleared from the unplowed field. They sat like soldiers guarding the entrance to the woods. Their tops were covered with snow. As I passed them, I expected to see my father coming toward me, pulling the horses and the wood sled. But I didn't. I knew he wouldn't have forgotten about the *Silver Dart*, but maybe he had lost track of time. After a while, I thought I might hear the sound of his axe cutting into a tree, but the woods were perfectly quiet. The only sounds I heard were the crunch of my boots and my breath.

I was surprised how far my father had gone into the woods. Now I was really worried we were going to miss the flight. I stopped again, held my breath and listened for the sound of his axe. But there was nothing but silence. That was strange; he couldn't have gone *that* far. And then, in a little gully, I saw the horses. They were harnessed to the sled and standing still. But there was no wood on the sled and no sign of my father. Where was he?

"Dad? Dad?" My voice echoed through the woods. Then I thought I heard a muffled voice. It sounded like it was coming from behind a tree that was lying on the ground. I went closer to the tree and saw my father's boots sticking out. He was under the tree!

I raced to the other side of the tree. My father was down in the snow, and the tree was on top of him. "Dad! Are you hurt?"

My father turned his head slowly and looked at me. He spoke, but his voice was weak with shivering. "Eddie. God bless you, my son. I'm stuck. The tree fell the wrong way. I was in too much of a hurry. I didn't cut it right. I was trying to get to the lake...." He winced with pain. I came and knelt beside him. "Dad, are you going to be all right? Can I dig you out?"

"I think I'll be all right. My chest and legs are sore. I'm just pinned. And I'm cold. I think maybe my arm's broke. The tree hit me and knocked me down. But it's not resting on me, thank God, it's resting on that log there." He pointed with his head. "If it slips off that log.... Heaven forbid."

"What should I do? Should I go get help?"

My father grinned, then winced with pain. "Everybody's gone down to the lake. And that's too far, Eddie. I'd freeze to death by the time you got back."

"Can't I dig you out?"

"No, it's all rocky ground underneath me. And it's frozen. You can't dig it."

"Can I cut the tree?"

"My son, it would take you all day to cut through this tree. And the cutting would probably shake it off that log, and that would finish me."

"Dad, what should we do? Tell me what to do." I was really worried now.

"Do you know if McLeary went to the lake, too?"

"I don't know."

"He could help, I think. He's an awfully strong man."

As I stared at my father trapped under the tree, I tried to think of the smartest thing to do. I took off my jacket and hat.

"What are you doing, Eddie? Put your hat back on. Put your jacket on."

I reached down and pulled my hat onto my father's head. "You need it more than me, Dad." Then I wrapped my jacket around his shoulders and tied the arms in front of his neck to keep his face warm.

"Eddie?"

"I'm going to run home and down to Mr. McLeary as fast as I can. I'll be right back, Dad. I'll get help."

"Eddie?"

"Just wait, Dad. I'm going as fast as I can."

My father just dropped his head and nodded. I took off as fast as I could through the snow. I followed the horses' tracks back to the farm. The horses would not have been any faster through the woods with all the snow. It was hard running in the snow, and I was out of breath, but I wasn't cold. I didn't bother going into the house because there was nobody there. I kept going right down the hill toward the McLeary farm. I just hoped and prayed that Mr. McLeary was home.

There was no one at the house, so I ran into the barn. "Mr. McLeary? Mr. McLeary?" There was no answer. I got such a sinking feeling then. My father was trapped in the woods, and I was all alone. Everyone was down at the lake, but if I went all the way down there and back, my father would freeze to death. I had to rescue him by myself *now*. But how? The only thing I could think of was to lift the tree off of him. At least that was something I knew how to do.

I raced into the room where Mr. McLeary kept his rope and pulleys. I pulled them down onto the floor and ran out and searched for a sled. I found one leaning against the outside of the barn. I grabbed the rope and pulleys and threw them onto the sled. Then I pulled the sled up the hill. It was a lot easier than carrying them. Back at our house, I ran in and grabbed my father's heavy winter coat that he wore to church, then grabbed the rope, pulleys and chains from our barn, threw them onto the sled and headed back into the woods. It was the middle of the afternoon now, but you could already feel the twilight coming. I knew that the flight had taken place already or was taking place right now. But I didn't care.

My father was shivering even more when I returned. His lips were blue. He looked sleepy, and his voice was very weak.

"Dad! Dad!" I shoved his jacket in behind him as far as I could get it and pulled it around his shoulders and down over his head. He looked up at me almost as if he didn't recognize me.

"Eddie. . . ."

"I'm going to raise the tree, Dad, and pull you out. Just hold on, Dad. Just hold on."

I threw the chains around one end of the tree. Then I climbed up the strongest tree that was close to the fallen tree and tied two pulleys around it. I tied them about fifteen feet off the ground. Then I chose four more trees and tied a pulley around each, as fast as I could, so that each of the two ropes would run through three pulleys. The distance wasn't as far as when we were pulling stones from the field, so I was able to use just two ropes. I climbed the tree again and fitted the ropes through the first two pulleys. Then I climbed down, tied the ropes to the chains and fitted the other ends through the rest of the pulleys. I unhooked the horses from the wood sled, brought them around and tied the ropes to their harnesses. We were ready. I checked on my father one last time. He was trying to tell me something, but was shivering so badly I couldn't make out what he was saying.

"Eddie...."

"I'm going to raise the tree now, Dad."

I ran around and made one last check before picking up the horses' leads and pulling on them. The horses came forward, and the tree rose into the air like a toothpick. I quickly tied the leads together around a tree so the horses couldn't back up and drop the fallen tree. Then I ran back to my father.

The hardest thing was pulling him out and getting him onto the sled. He was so weak he couldn't even stand. And he was so cold that he was confused, and I had to tell him what to do, which was the strangest feeling in the world. I had to tell him when to move his feet and where to put his arms. Once he was on the sled, I untied the horses' leads and backed them up until the fallen tree was down again. Then I harnessed the horses to the sled and led them out of the woods. I left the pulleys and rope behind. We could get them later.

My mother came running when she saw me pulling the horses across the field. When she saw my father lying on the sled and not moving, she screamed and started crying. That brought my sister and brother running. Together, the four of us helped my father into the house. Then my mother sent my sister and me for the doctor. It was long past dark when we finally returned, and my father was fast asleep. While the doctor examined him, my mother gave me some supper. I sat down at the table exhausted and hungry.

"He's going to be all right," said my mother. "The doctor said so."

My brother and sister sat at the table, too, even though they had already eaten.

"I'm sorry you didn't get to see the *Silver Dart* fly," said my brother.

"Yeah, me too," I said.

"It was amazing. I'm going to be a pilot like Douglas McCurdy when I grow up."

"We met Mr. Bell," said my sister. "He's really nice, just like you said."

"I know."

"It's too bad you didn't get to see the *Silver Dart* fly," said my brother again.

"Well, you can't have everything," I said as I ate my supper. "Anyway, I'm celebrating my successes."

"What?" My brother looked confused.

"Never mind," I said. "I will explain it to you when you're older."

Chapter 23

My father suffered a broken arm, three broken ribs, a bruised stomach and badly bruised legs. Doctor Chisholm said that he would be fine after he rested for a couple of weeks, but he had to stay in bed and eat lots of chicken soup. It was lucky I had found him when I did, the doctor said, because my father was also suffering from hypothermia and would not have survived if he had been in the woods much longer. If I had gone down to the lake to watch the flight of the *Silver Dart*, my father would have died.

My mother took good care of my father. She ran around the house finding things to make him more comfortable. And she said to me, "Thank the Lord above he gave you the brain that he did, or your father..." and then she almost started crying again.

I sat with my father the next day. He smiled and said that he was feeling a lot warmer but was mighty sore. He said he should have listened to his own best judgement and not hurried when he was cutting such a large tree. He told me I had acted like a man. I had made wise decisions and acted with courage and intelligence. He said he was proud of me. That felt really good. He said he was sorry that we didn't get to see the *Silver Dart* fly. Then he laughed and said that he couldn't believe he missed yet another chance to meet Mr. Bell. I said I was sorry, too.

A little while later we heard voices downstairs. My mother was greeting someone. Somebody had come to visit my father. From the sound of the voices, I was guessing it was Mr. McLeary. From the sound of the heavy feet on the stairs, I was certain it was Mr. McLeary. But when the door opened, there, standing tall and smiling like the friendliest person in the world, was Mr. Bell.

"Eddie!" said Mr. Bell, and he stuck out his hand.

I jumped up, crossed the room and shook his hand. "Hello, Mr. Bell."

Mr. Bell looked at my father on the bed, and his face grew grim. He came closer. "I heard there had been an accident. I hope everything is going to be all right."

My father tried to sit up on the bed, but it was too painful for him.

"Please, please..." said Mr. Bell, and he came to the edge of the bed.

"Mr. Bell," I said, "This is my father."

My father raised his hand, and Mr. Bell gripped it and shook it. "Pleased to meet you, Mr. MacDonald. You've got a terrific son here. A brilliant young man. I wish I could hire him." Mr. Bell looked at me and winked. My father smiled, and his eyes were shiny. "I'm pleased to meet you too, Sir. We are honoured to have you in our home."

This was the first and only time I ever heard my father call another man "Sir."

"Well, when I didn't see Eddie down at the lake yesterday, I knew something was amiss. I had to come and see for myself that everything was okay."

"I'm sorry we missed the flight of your flying machine," said my father.

"Me too," I said.

"Ah, it was a great flight," said Mr. Bell. "The *Silver Dart* flew just like an eagle over the lake. But don't you worry in the least; she's flying again this afternoon, and tomorrow, and a good number of times after that if Douglas has his way, which I have no doubt he will. And that reminds me, I'd better get myself back down to the lake or he'll fly it without me."

"Will you go up in the aeroplane, Mr. Bell?" I asked.

Mr. Bell turned toward me with a look of horror. Then he burst out laughing. "What? Me? Hah, hah, hah! Heavens, no! The machine would never get off the ground with me on board!" Then he slapped his belly. I couldn't help smiling. Mr. Bell was so funny when he wanted to be. Then he leaned closer to my father and grew serious again. "Rest well, my dear man."

My father nodded his head and smiled back. "I will do that, Sir. And thank you for doing us the honour of visiting us in our home."

"No trouble at all," said Mr. Bell. He pulled out his watch, squinted at it and said that he had to go. He raised his hand and waved as if we were standing across a field. Then he went out the door. I followed him down the stairs. My mother was standing in the kitchen with a warm smile on her face. "Can I offer you a cup of tea, Mr. Bell?"

"I would love a cup of tea, indeed, Mrs. MacDonald, but I'm afraid I've got to get myself down to the lake or I'll miss the second flight of the *Silver Dart*, and I wouldn't want to do that."

"No, Sir," said my mother. "It was kind of you to visit."

"A pleasure," said Mr. Bell, and he tipped his head to my mother, picked up his coat and cap and went out the door. I followed him.

There was a man waiting with a team of horses and a sleigh. Mr. Bell slapped my shoulder and climbed onto the sleigh. "You did a great job reading the book, my boy."

I took a deep breath. "I wasn't really reading it. I just memorized it. I still can't read much yet."

Mr. Bell took out his pipe and lit it. I could tell that he was thinking. After he took the first puff, he squinted at me through the smoke. "You and I are a pair, Eddie. Reading and inventing. When the world tells us we can't do something, it only makes us work harder! Success might come slowly, and it might feel at times as though it will never come. But sure as day follows night, it will. And that's because we never give up. You wrote me a darn good letter. And you made a terrific presentation to your class. Don't forget to celebrate those successes."

The sleigh started to pull away. Mr. Bell waved. "Celebrate your successes, my boy!"

"I will! Goodbye, Mr. Bell!"

Epilogue

The *Silver Dart* roared on the ice like a monster from another world. I had no idea it would be so loud. I couldn't hear anything but its roar. It sounded like it was announcing to the whole world that everything really was about to change. Seeing it and hearing it made me believe that.

Douglas McCurdy sat inside the aeroplane. I saw the concentrated look on his face, and I bet he didn't even notice the cold. Mr. Bell sat in his sleigh with Mrs. Bell, wrapped in furs. He wore his most serious expression. He waved his arm, and Mr. McCurdy waved back. Some men who were holding the aeroplane down, as if it were a wild horse, let it go, and the machine started to roll. It rolled quickly around, straightened itself out as if it had a mind of its own and started down the ice. For a little while, I had the feeling it was just going to ride all the way across the lake, and that would have been interesting to watch, too. But the aeroplane suddenly jumped into the air. It lifted off the ground as if it didn't weigh anything at all. Then it went higher and faster. Everyone on the ice cheered. The aeroplane went down toward Beinn

Bhreagh, turned around in the air and came back. It was unbelievable. As it passed over our heads, Mr. McCurdy stuck out his hand and waved. I waved back. Then he kept going until he was out of sight. I stared at the sky and watched him disappear. I couldn't take my eyes away. I couldn't even blink. It was hard to believe he could travel so far away so quickly.

A little while later, he came back. You could hear the aeroplane coming from far away. It sounded like a mosquito at first. But it got louder and louder until you couldn't even hear yourself cheering. It was so exciting. I was thrilled. It was the greatest thing I would ever see in my whole life.

That night, before I went to bed, I sat at my desk with my father's dictionary and a pencil and paper. Slowly and carefully, I wrote out these words:

Dear Miss Keller,

Today, I watched the Silver Dart fly. It was the most amazing thing I ever saw. I am going to try to tell you what it looked like....

The End

Philip Roy keeps residence in two places these days, running back and forth between his hometown, Antigonish, Nova Scotia, and his adopted town, St. Marys, Ontario. Continuing to write adventurous and historical young adult novels focusing on social, environmental, and global concerns, he is also excited to be presenting his first picture book: *Mouse Tales*, the first volume in the Happy the Pocket Mouse series (Ronsdale Press), coming out in the new year.

In 2012, Philip published the historical novel *Blood Brothers in Louisbourg* (CBU Press). In 2013, along with *Me & Mr. Bell*, Philip will be bringing out the sixth volume in the Submarine Outlaw series, *Seas of South Africa* (Ronsdale Press).

Besides writing, travelling and running in the woods and countryside of Nova Scotia and Ontario, Philip spends his time composing music. His first score, for the Nova Scotia-based film *The Seer*, by Gary Blackwood (FLAWed Productions), will be produced in 2013. Philip is also collaborating with Gary Blackwood on an opera, *The Mad Doctor*.

Philip's website is philiproy.ca.